F
Coldsmith

Coldsmith, Don
  Walks in the Sun

4/30/92   **DATE DUE**

JUL 02 '92	JUN 01 2004	
AUG 28 '92	DEC 09 2004	
DEC 15 '9?	FEB 16 2005	
APR 12 '93	MAY 23 2005	
JUL 17 '93	AUG 04 2005 JD	
JUL 07 '94	DEC 19 2005	
FEB 11 '95	JUN 13 2006	
JAN 03 '96	9-1-06	
JAN 29 '96	DEC 15 09	
APR 03 '96	OCT 15 '10	
OCT 13 1998	11-1-11	
FEB 22 2000		
JUL 05 2000		
JUL 17 2002		
SEP 27 2002		
10-1-03		

#47-0108 Peel Off Pressure Sensitive

T 28262

HESSTON PUBLIC LIBRARY
WITHDRAWN
P.O. BOX 640
HESSTON, KANSAS 67062

WALKS IN THE SUN

ALSO BY DON COLDSMITH

RETURN OF THE SPANISH

BRIDE OF THE MORNING STAR

QUEST FOR THE WHITE BULL

FORT DE CHASTAIGNE

SONG OF THE ROCK

TRAIL FROM TAOS

THE FLOWER IN THE MOUNTAINS

THE MEDICINE KNIFE

RETURN TO THE RIVER

RIVER OF SWANS

PALE STAR

THE SACRED HILLS

MOON OF THUNDER

DAUGHTER OF THE EAGLE

MAN OF THE SHADOWS

FOLLOW THE WIND

THE ELK-DOG HERITAGE

BUFFALO MEDICINE

TRAIL OF THE SPANISH BIT

THE CHANGING WIND

THE TRAVELER

WORLD OF SILENCE

THE SMOKY HILL

HESSTON PUBLIC LIBRARY
110 E. SMITH
P.O. BOX 640
HESSTON, KANSAS 67062

F
Coldsmith
27965
28262

WALKS IN THE SUN

Don Coldsmith

BANTAM BOOKS
NEW YORK • TORONTO • LONDON • SYDNEY • AUCKLAND

WALKS IN THE SUN

A Bantam Book / April 1992

All rights reserved.

Copyright © 1992 by Don Coldsmith.

Book design and illustrations by Richard Oriolo.
Map designed by GDS / Jeffrey L. Ward.

No part of this book may be reproduced or transmitted in any form or by any means, electronic or mechanical, including photocopying, recording, or by any information storage and retrieval system, without permission in writing from the publisher.
For information address: Bantam Books.

Library of Congress Cataloging-in-Publication Data
Coldsmith, Don, 1926–
    Walks in the sun : a novel / by Don Coldsmith.
        p.   cm.
    ISBN 0–553–08262–0
    1. Indians of North America—Fiction.   I. Title.
PS3553.O445W35   1992
813'.54—dc20   91–35210
                                                                          CIP

Published simultaneously in the United States and Canada

Bantam Books are published by Bantam Books, a division of Bantam Doubleday Dell Publishing Group, Inc. Its trademark, consisting of the words "Bantam Books" and the portrayal of a rooster, is Registered in U.S. Patent and Trademark Office and in other countries. Marca Registrada. Bantam Books, 666 Fifth Avenue, New York, New York 10103.

PRINTED IN THE UNITED STATES OF AMERICA

BVG   0   9   8   7   6   5   4   3   2   1

To Robert Conley,
who planted the seed for the idea
from which this book sprouted.

Introduction

▼▼▼

It is known that many Native Americans traveled widely from earliest times, trading and exploring. People of the plains knew of a salty ocean far to the east, and some from the southeast had seen the Rocky Mountains. Prehistoric trails crisscrossed the continent. Undoubtedly such exploration became even more common with easier travel after the coming of the horse in the sixteenth and seventeenth centuries. Many tribes have legends of these explorations.

This story is suggested, although distantly, by a similar expedition carried out by a party of Kiowas in a bygone century. However, this does not pretend to be their story. There are major differences, and no similarity to actual persons is intended.

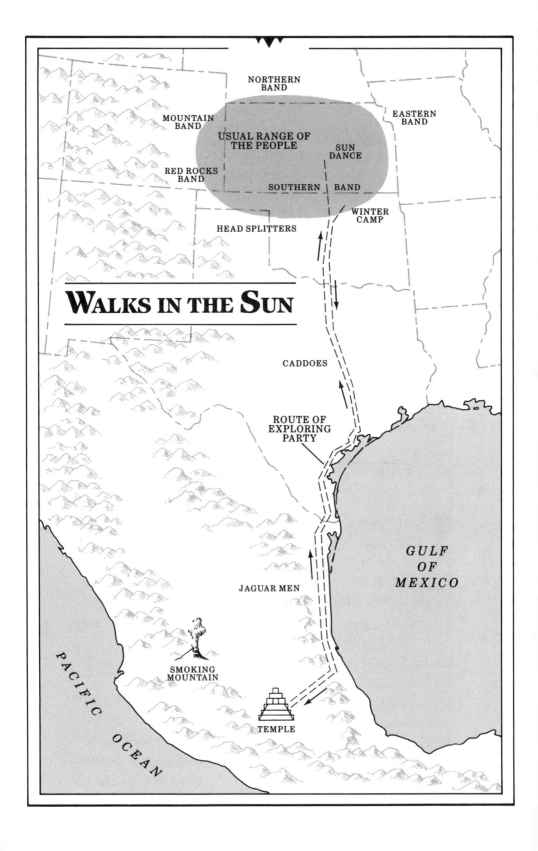

WALKS IN THE SUN

Time period: circa 1720s

1

The People had gathered for the Sun Dance, held each season in the Moon of Roses. As always, it was a time of great jubilation, a combination of religious festival, social event, politics, and a reunion of the far-flung bands of the nation.

The five bands had gathered and had made their camps in the traditionally assigned areas. The Northern and Southern bands, of course, in their respective directions from the ring of the Big Council. The Eastern band camped in a position to the northeast. Due east was reserved for the Sun to enter, just as the door of a lodge must face the east.

Just south of Sun Boy's opening, a place was reserved for an almost forgotten band. Its original name had been lost, and now it was usually referred to as the Lost band. Its people had all been killed many generations ago, it was said, by an enemy in the north. Their camping place and their place in the Council ring was still reserved, in case any descendants of possible survivors should ever show up to claim their birthright.

The westward limits of the range of the People were marked by the territory of the Mountain band and the Red Rocks.

All bands were now gathered, and the construction of the Medicine Lodge was in progress. It would be a few days yet until all was ready. Then the announcement would be made, and the days of preparatory ritual would begin.

Meanwhile, the social occasion was in full swing. Women visited and gossiped and renewed old friendships. Old men smoked and chatted and dreamed of younger times. Young people flirted or played traditional games and contests, wagering on the outcome, or raced horses and bet on those.

The warrior societies in their distinctive garb and facial paint held their ceremonies and inductions and special dances. The entire festival was without rival in the world of the People.

This season, one of the major topics of conversation was that of the fate of the Southern band. It was the second Sun Dance since the political squabble that had torn the band apart. Some of their warriors were still missing, and there were lodges empty of their men. One or two of the women had remarried after the prescribed period of mourning for a missing husband.

"Well, Blue Jay was always a little crazy," one of the old men said. "His grandmother was of the Eastern band, you know."

There was a chuckle at the old ethnic joke. The Eastern band had always been known for foolish ways. There were

2

constant jokes, and it must be said that there were those in the Eastern band who relished the notoriety, and told such jokes on themselves. (But what could one expect?)

And the others . . . It was not unusual for someone with a lame horse to be given advice: "Keep it! Maybe you can sell it to the Eastern band at the Sun Dance."

But everyone knew that this situation was serious. Such a jibe about their leader had too many dark overtones to be really enjoyed. It had been a long time since Blue Jay had led his little group of loyal followers on the scouting trip to the south.

It was a simple thing to have argued about with the leaders of the Southern band: where to make winter camp. Broken Lance, the aging band chief, had chosen a site not to the liking of Blue Jay. This popular and volatile young subchief had political ambitions, and it was common gossip that he took every opportunity to criticize those in authority. His style leaned to extremes, and his warrior membership choice was that of the Bloods, the most radical of the societies. This society, born in political turmoil generations ago, had always attracted a slightly erratic type of young man. Those who outgrew the impetuousness of youth sometimes matured into great leaders, because their followers possessed a fierce loyalty. Followers of Blue Jay, it was said, would go anywhere, fight anyone or anything, if he asked it.

The scouting party had been gone for two winters now, and the chances that they survived seemed slim. Blue Jay had announced, after the establishment of the winter camp that autumn, that he proposed to explore to the south, where a warmer climate would favor a more comfortable season.

"But you would be leaving the country of the People," some argued. "Who knows what lies beyond?"

"There is grass there, too," Blue Jay retorted. "The

buffalo make their winter camp somewhere to the south. Maybe we should follow *them.*"

"But the People do not know that country."

"They will," Blue Jay snapped, "when I return."

Ten men had followed him. Eleven in all, well armed and with provisions, rode out that day in the Moon of Falling Leaves and had not returned. Old Broken Lance said nothing. He would not dignify the expedition by his comment.

There had been much discussion at the Sun Dance last season. Many had expected Blue Jay and his party to make a showy arrival during the festival, to gain political prestige. Many others, however, shook their heads. Old women clucked their tongues and pointed out that there was already an empty place in the Council circle, in honor of a now extinct band of long ago. They, too, had had a foolish leader.

This year, it was a general opinion that the missing party would not return. There was less said about it, and it was apparent that the wives of the missing men were subjected to more vigorous courtship by potential husbands. Already, one young woman had moved into the lodge of her sister as a second wife.

It was very surprising when one of the wolves, the mounted scouts who constantly circled the encampment to watch for the unexpected, rode in at a hard gallop, shouting the news.

"Blue Jay is back!"

The word spread, like a prairie fire in the springtime. People gathered quickly, shouting questions: *Where? How near?* And the one most pressing: *How many others?*

"They are just over the hill." The excited wolf pointed.

There was a rush by the young men to catch horses and ride to escort the returning warriors.

"Only two," the scout continued, his tone more subdued.

4

"Blue Jay and Walks in the Sun. Their faces are painted."

A wail of anguish rose from a young woman in the crowd. Her husband had been with Blue Jay, and the painted faces, signifying mourning, told a grim story. The others of the party were dead. Someone led the young woman away, and the word spread quickly. The plaintive wails of the Song of Mourning began to rise here and there.

The crowd was growing to meet the returning men. The two riders entered the camp, flanked by the wolves and the young men who had ridden out as an escort. As they drew near, the noise and shouting died, replaced by an awed silence at the appearance of the two. Both were thin, their garments tattered and clumsily patched. But the real shock was in the comparison of the two.

Blue Jay, the flamboyant leader, was clearly a broken man. His hair was snowy white, his face was drawn, and his posture on the horse showed clearly that his body was racked with disease. His eyes burned with an intense glassy stare, as if they did not see, and he seemed unable to speak.

Walks in the Sun drew his horse to a stop and looked around the crowd. He, too, showed the ravages of illness, but it was apparent that he was in far better condition than his companion.

"I have brought Blue Jay home," he stated.

There was a flurry of excited questions, but he shrugged them off.

"We must rest," he protested. "I will tell you all of it, when we have eaten and slept."

He slid wearily from his horse, and his wife rushed forward to embrace him. She had always insisted that he would return. Running Deer was one of the most beautiful of women, and she had spurned several would-be suitors during her husband's absence. Now, she flew into his arms, smothering him with kisses and with tears of joy.

Blue Jay's wife had also come forward, but more cautiously, as if she did not even recognize the returnee. It was well-known that she had become quite friendly with a handsome young man of the Red Rocks band. She could not be blamed for that, though she now had a difficult problem. She and others helped Blue Jay to dismount and led him quietly away, as one would a child. It was apparent that whatever prestige this young man had once held, it was now gone.

And just as surely, the prestige of Walks in the Sun had risen. He had been able not only to survive, but to bring home his fallen leader. Here was a young man who was already highly respected. His name had been chosen by his mother, who had insisted since his birth that he would become a great man. That, of course, was not unusual. Does not every mother think this of her son?

But he *had* appeared to have special gifts from the time he was small. He could predict the results of the toss in the games of the plumstones. Yet he considered this unimportant, and seemed to realize quite early that this gift was not to be used for his own gain.

He was often a loner, a deep thinker, and it was no surprise to those who knew him when he apprenticed himself to the holy man.

"He has a powerful gift," the old medicine man told the youngster's parents. "And, I am made to think that he is named well. He does, indeed, walk in sunlight."

There had been many who were surprised when the young holy man chose to join the exploring party of Blue Jay. Though the two had been friends since childhood, it was plain that their paths were divergent.

"Blue Jay is crazy!" scolded the holy man. "Why would you follow *him*?"

"Maybe *because* he is crazy," answered Walks in the Sun quietly. "Maybe it will be that I can help him. And he is my friend."

The old man nodded.

"It is as you say. If you are made to think so, you should go."

Running Deer, too, understood what he must do. She did not necessarily approve, but in the few years that they had been married she had learned that he must follow the urge of his spirit-guide. It was not necessary to know the reason.

Perhaps it was this same understanding that led her to her firm conviction that he would return. And now, he had. She was eager to hear his story. But she would wait, like the others. It was important first that he eat and rest. As it happened, he fell into the deep sleep of exhaustion almost before he finished eating.

"Come," she whispered to their daughter. "We will let him sleep."

They quietly left the lodge, and she took the child to the lodge of her parents. Then she returned and lay down on the soft sleeping-robe beside her husband. He was snoring softly, and it was good. Much as she wished to, she would not disturb him. She would only stay beside him and watch until he woke.

By the time shadows began to lengthen, it was common knowledge that there would be a story fire at the ring of the Big Council. The ceremonial days of the Sun Dance had not yet been announced, so the ritual countdown had not begun. Here would be an exciting addition to the gathering, a report from the survivors of the ill-fated expedition.

Word had already spread that the confused Blue Jay was babbling about supernatural creatures and evil spirits. But the wife of Blue Jay also said that he would be unable to participate in the story fire. His illness had drawn too much from his weakened body, and he must rest. Walks in the Sun would tell their story.

Of course, the People already assumed this. He had spoken for the two on their arrival. And Sun was a good speaker.

The crowd gathered early, to make sure of good seats. As darkness fell, the fire was lighted, and the dusky shadows were pushed back, enlarging the circle of light. A log burned in two and fell into the heart of the fire. It sent a shower of sparks up into the blackness of the night sky, to mingle with the stars for a moment before they died.

Then came Walks in the Sun, walking beside his wife. He had bathed and changed, and now wore new buckskins that Running Deer had been saving for his return. The crowd quieted as he strode forward and began to speak.

"As you know, my friends, any story of the People begins with Creation. We came from the world inside the Earth, which is dark and sunless, crawling through the hollow log at the beckoning of Sun Boy. A good storyteller would tell of these things in detail, and of Fat Woman who became stuck in the log. But I am tired, and you wish to hear of our journey."

There were nods of approval.

"So, I will be brief, also, in the mention of the People's journey from the north to seek a better climate. That, too, was long ago, many lifetimes, when the People came to the Sacred Hills and called them home. We wander, we raise our lodges in other places, but our Sun Dance, which unites all the bands each season, always takes place somewhere in the Sacred Hills. It is here that the grasses are nourished with the blood, flesh, and bones of our ancestors. Here, we celebrate the return of the sun, the grass, and the buffalo. Forgive me, my friends . . . my voice trembles and becomes halting, and tears come to my eyes. I am grateful to be home. . . ."

There was a sympathetic silence, a few nods of understanding. Walks in the Sun took a deep breath and continued.

"Then, many generations later, the coming of the horse. The First Elk-dog, as you remember, was ridden by Heads-Off, the outsider who joined our Southern band. His blood flows in the veins of many of us."

Even Walks in the Sun could not miss the opportunity to mention this, the most prestigious event in the history of his own band. He paused a moment for effect. He was a much more skilled storyteller than he pretended, and his showmanship would not let him overlook this opportunity. After just the right interval, he resumed his account.

"You remember, two seasons ago, you of the Southern band . . . I suppose all the People have heard, now. The quarrel . . . no, not a quarrel, a disagreement, between two of our leaders. It was over such a simple thing, I am made to think as I look back . . . where is the winter camp to be? Our leader, Broken Lance, chose the place, as is proper, and the young men followed his counsel, though they had disagreed. This, too, is proper."

Walks in the Sun, ever the diplomat, was being cautious in his depiction of the political falling-out. It would not do to leave an unhealed wound among the People over this tragedy. Broken Lance sat quietly, dignified and stoic, willing to let others do the healing.

"Some of the young men," Walks in the Sun continued, "led by our brother Blue Jay, decided to explore to the south to find what sort of winter camp we might try at some later time. I was made to think that I should go, too. Blue Jay and his party would be among unfamiliar spirits, so should not a man of the spirit, a holy man, be with them? It is true that my family was not completely happy that I was called to this."

There were chuckles of understanding. The firm quality of this marriage was well-known.

"Running Deer wished to go, too. But, it had already been decided that there would be only men. A few days, maybe even weeks, and back to winter camp before Cold Maker's arrival. So, we planned our departure. Blue Jay was leader, our tracker was Snake-Road, and I would be their spiritual counsel. We had also some excellent bowmen, and some who used the lance. All were well mounted. It was, you see, a well-planned exploring party."

He wanted no doubt of that, no blame on anyone. There was no point now in any bitterness or recrimination. It was over, and it was time for healing to begin.

"Now," he stated very formally, "I will tell you of our experiences. This part is our story."

There was complete silence, and every eye was fixed upon him as Walks in the Sun began his tragic tale.

"My brothers and sisters, it is good to be home, here with you in the Sacred Hills and away from the monstrous things we have seen. I will tell you of those later. We have seen much, both good and evil. But know this before I begin: We went *too far* south!"

2

At first, there was nothing out of the ordinary. We were in familiar country, grassland spotted with areas of oak thickets. Good country in which to winter. Blue Jay led us south and a little west. We did not want to go too far west, because winter in the shortgrass country is hard, and an early snow could surprise us.

But the weather was good, a fine Second Summer. It was enjoyable, and I thought that it was good, a good way for young men to make their feelings known about the winter camp, yet do no harm, and have some fun, besides.

After about five sleeps, Snake-Road called us to notice

that it seemed no later in the season than when we left the band. It was as if time stood still, though the sun had risen and set several times. We talked of this around the fire that night. Someone noted that the moon showed that time *was* going on. It was rising later each night. When we left the band, the moon was just past full. Now, it was only half there, and did not rise until far into the night. So, we asked each other, why does the moon change, but not the sun? It was a great question.

Partly, I knew the answer because I had been watching the plants. Some are the same, of course, as they are here. I was interested because of the plants that are used for my medicine. Those and others. I was noticing that the ripening of some seeds, the falling of some leaves, were just happening in that area, but had already done so here before we left the band.

We know, of course, that the winter is milder to the south. That is why we winter there. Why the buffalo migrate, and the geese, and—but never mind, you know of these things.

But as we talked around the fire, we began to wonder. We were traveling, it seemed, about as fast as the season. A little faster, maybe. What would happen, someone asked, if one continued to ride south? Would he reach a spot where the season turned to meet him, and started back north? Maybe the buffalo know this, and turn around to start back each season, in midwinter.

"When?" asked another. "In the Moon of Long Nights? The Moon of Snows? That would be stupid."

"But think!" Blue Jay answered him. "In such a place, there would *be* no Moon of Snows." He then turned to me. "What do you think, holy man?"

"I do not know," I told him honestly. "I am made to think

that there is a limit somewhere. Of its nature, I cannot say. We have never been sure how far the buffalo go to winter."

"Some winter at home," another man said.

"That is true," said Blue Jay, "but only a few."

"Look," Snake-Road said, "we know that Cold Maker's lodge is an ice cave far to the north, no?"

"So it is said."

"Then there, it is *always* winter?"

We nodded, wondering what he was getting at.

"Well," he went on, "if there is a place of Never-Summer, should there not be another, of *Never-Winter?*"

We all looked at each other, and no one had an answer. Cold Maker, of course, is probably only a legend, but is a handy way to think of the far north. I was startled over this. The People have spent so many lifetimes fighting for survival against "Cold Maker" . . . have we made him more than he is? What if we could merely move *where he cannot go*? To the *south*.

True, it would mean leaving the Sacred Hills, but. . . . Forgive me, friends . . . the tears try to fill my eyes. You must realize that as we talked so, times were good, we were comfortable, and well fed. A place of Never-Winter sounded good to us. We could go back north to *summer* in our Sacred Hills. As someone said, we follow the buffalo, let us follow them farther.

I was uneasy about it. If this was a good thing, surely since Creation somebody would have discovered it. But, at the time, I have to admit, it sounded good, even to me. So good, I am afraid, that I was not listening to my spirit-guide. He would have warned me. . . .

Maybe the thing that was the greatest evil just then was that we encountered a hunting party of Head Splitters.

They are our allies, of course, and as soon as we recognized each other it was a day of joy.

"Greetings, our brothers," said their leader, using hand-signs as well as our tongue. Some Head Splitters speak our language quite well, you know, but this one was only fair at it.

We camped together, about the same number in our party as in theirs. They had meat, and we all feasted well. We talked of many things. The weather, the hunting, where our Sun Dance would be next year. The Head Splitters sometimes like to attend, you know, because they have no such ceremony of their own. And, that is good.

Then Blue Jay began to ask many questions about their customs. I did not quite understand why for a little while, but then I saw. The Head Splitters range farther to the south and west than we do, and Jay was asking of the southern extent of their area.

"Do you know how far the buffalo go to winter?" he finally asked.

"No," the Head Splitter replied. "Everyone winters somewhere. . . . Why?"

Blue Jay then explained to him of our observations about the seasons, and that we had wondered about a Never-Winter Place. They nodded.

"It is said that there is such a place," they told us.

"*Aiee!* Where?"

They were vague about that, pointing southward.

"Do your people go there?" asked Blue Jay.

"No, there seems no good reason. It is far, my friends, and there are dangers. . . ."

"Enemies?"

"No . . . well, maybe. Caddoes . . . Spanish. We trade with them, sometimes. But the country is hard."

"Harder than the prairie winter?" asked Blue Jay.

Everyone laughed.

Now, I was wearing the Elk-dog bit, which was used in the mouth of the First Horse by Heads-Off. As you all know, it is one of the most powerful of the medicines of the People. It has been handed down since White Buffalo learned that its circle enables control of the horse. I was made its keeper when I finished my apprenticeship . . . a great honor.

I had had a worrisome choice to make, when I decided to go with Blue Jay. My purpose would be to offer advice and counsel, and to try to foretell trouble or good. I did not really want to risk harm to so powerful an emblem. But it might be that I would need its power. Also, if I left it behind, who would care for it?

In the end, I decided to carry it, to use its power if we needed it. The easiest and safest way is to wear it, so that is what I was doing that night. Suddenly, the leader of the Head Splitters seemed to realize its significance.

"Holy man," he said, "you wear an amulet. Is that the Elk-dog medicine of your people?"

I nodded that it was, and there was a gasp from the Head Splitters. They moved to see better as I held it to let the firelight sparkle from its silver dangles. It is very impressive, of course.

One of the Head Splitters, a thoughtful man who had not said much, now spoke.

"Then this is a *medicine quest*?"

There was another gasp from the Head Splitters, and some of our men swaggered a little, pretending that this was our purpose all along. The Head Splitters began to treat us with even more honor and respect, and it felt good. No one bothered to deny that this was our purpose, even I,

I am sorry to say. Maybe this unearned pride was to cause . . . but never mind.

By the end of the evening when we sought our robes, I think most of us had convinced ourselves that it *was* a medicine quest. Surely Blue Jay believed it. From that time on, he seemed to believe that he had been called to lead this important quest. And I must confess, I thought so too, at that time. I was proud to be the adviser to the leader who was chosen for such a quest. I should have cast the bones, or consulted some of my other gifts, but I did not. Pride causes blindness sometimes. . . . Forgive me, my friends. Tears come easily tonight. A moment . . .

Well . . . After we had convinced ourselves that it *was* a medicine quest, and that we were a chosen group, we asked the Head Splitters for more detail about the land to the south. They were happy to tell us. It was grassland, they said, for many sleeps south. All the way, in fact, to a great salty body of water, an ocean. There we would find many strange things to see.

"Is it always summer at this salty water?" I asked.

"Pretty much. So the Caddoes say. They live in grass lodges."

"*Aiee!* In the winter?" asked someone.

Blue Jay was skeptical. "Have you been there?" he asked. "Any of you?"

The Head Splitters looked from one to the other, and it seemed that no one had been. We all laughed. They had been telling us of things which they did not really know, either. But some things they *did* know.

"Should we go straight south, or southwest?" asked Blue Jay.

They conferred a little in their own tongue, and then

gave what we took to be good advice. Head Splitters do know some of that southwest country.

"If you go straight south, you stay mostly in grassland. Southwest, you would get into Spanish territory. A little more south than west takes you to the great canyon, the place of Hard Trees, which the Spanish call Palo Duro."

"Yes. Our people call it the Hole-in-the-Ground. Our holy man found the White Bull there."

"Yes, that is true. You know it, then."

"We know of it," answered Blue Jay. "None of us have been there."

"You wish to go? We can tell you the way."

"No," said Blue Jay. "That is not the purpose of our quest."

You see, he had already convinced himself that this was an important medicine quest.

"I am made to think," Jay went on, "that we should go on straight south, to the Salt Water."

Even his followers were surprised, but excited at this prospect. I was, too, I admit it.

"How far? How many sleeps?" we asked the Head Splitters.

They did not really know, but told us anyway, because they wanted to help us.

"Maybe a moon . . . maybe more."

"It is good!" announced Blue Jay, as if it was all he needed. "We can be back with our families by the Moon of Long Nights."

Somehow, that seemed to make sense. It could not really be done that quickly, but we did not know that, then. It is hard to be realistic about the unknown when you are warm and comfortable and your bellies are full and there are pleasant companions. I hope you will understand how it was, my friends, how all of us could be so wrong. *Aiee*, the tears come again. . . .

Next morning, we parted from the pleasant company of our Head Splitter friends. One of them, a very good man named Bear's Head, offered to go with us. He knew the tongue of the Caddoes, and could be of help to us. They used some hand-signs, he said, but not as fluently as those of us from the tallgrass prairie.

Some of our men were a little concerned over how his name came to be. Bear's Head . . . for a Head Splitter to kill a bear, or eat it, or cut off its head, is good. They eat bears, though the People do not. That is their way, and of no concern to us. But some disliked the use of the Bear's Head name, so we called him "Caddo Talker."

No matter . . . We were now twelve as we moved on to the south that day. All of us were convinced that we were taking part in a great quest that would affect the People for many generations.

3

When we left the Head Splitters and moved on, it was with a great sense of purpose. We had all convinced ourselves that this was a great, important thing that we were doing. As big for the People, maybe, as the coming of the horse. I have to admit, my friends, that I should have seen the dangers ahead. That was my purpose in being there. But I, too, was caught up in the excitement of the thing. I, too, believed in our quest. It is always easy to look back and say "I should have known," but we did not. In our defense, I would only say that the back trail is always plainer than the one ahead.

Then, too, I was possibly confused as I looked for signs. On the morning that we parted from the Head Splitters, I saw three crows fly to alight on a little ridge to the south of us. *Ah,* I thought, *what better sign?* The crow's power to assist in listening for the guidance of the spirit is well-known. And *three.* It seemed very good. I have wondered much of the meaning of this. Did I somehow misinterpret the sign? It seemed plain enough.

As I look back, I see a possibility or two. One, we were entering strange country. Maybe the signs are different in different places. Maybe in that country the three crows meant something else. In light of later events, this seems very likely. Or, maybe they were just crows, who happened there at that time.

Yet another thing comes to my mind, one that is a constant threat to any holy man. Was I, maybe, seeing in the signs what I *wished* to see? If so, I am guilty of misuse of my gift. But I was swayed by the lofty purpose of the quest. I *was* allowed to survive, so maybe . . . but enough. If we ever think we can understand all the things of the spirit, we have already missed the point. Some things are not meant to be understood.

So, we moved on southward, we twelve, counting Bear's Head, or Caddo Talker, as our men were now calling him. He was a pleasant companion, and told us much about the land we were crossing.

I had noticed plants of many sorts not known here, and we talked of those as we rode. There were grasses which seemed unlike ours. Where ours are tall and upright in the Sacred Hills, many of these seemed to creep upon the ground like our short buffalo grass, but heavier. Well, you would have to see it to understand. And, though most were now dry for the winter, it was plain that there were more hot-season grasses. The bushes, too, in brushy areas, were of types I had never seen. Many wore thorns. There has long been a saying among the People that in the desert, everything that grows carries a weapon. This was not desert, but a kind of dry grassland unfamiliar to us. More cactus, of several sorts. The fruit of one which Caddo Talker pointed out, he said was used as food. We did not know whether to believe him. There were times later when we would have welcomed a chance to try it.

In low places, where there may have been more moisture in the ground, there were heavy thickets of a sort of reed or giant stemmy grass, which grew maybe twice as tall as a man on a horse. Caddo Talker said we should avoid these places, because giant real-snakes made their lodges there. He was right, too. We saw one sleeping in the sun that must have been longer than a man is tall. I rode nearer to get a better look. It was fatter in the middle than my arm here above the elbow, and carried eleven or twelve rattles at its tail. My horse was alarmed, and I decided that she was right. I moved away. That real-snake seemed very dangerous at the time, but later we would have been happy to be faced with problems no greater. Real-snakes, we could understand.

We saw another creature at about that time . . . forgive me for telling in such detail. This is my function, my gift, to know the plants and animals. And it *is* important to the story.

This one was about the size of a possum. It looked like a possum, in fact, and acted like one. It was digging in an ant-lodge just at dusk, near our camp. It let us come quite near, though we were cautious. Now, hear this: this creature wore a bony shell, like a turtle. Not exactly . . . well, you know how the turtle's lower shell is jointed, so that he can go inside and close the door? Yes, this little animal's shell was jointed all over. When it became alarmed, it pulled in head, tail, and feet, and rolled itself into a hard round ball. Yes, it is true! We rolled it around a little to examine it.

Caddo Talker said that some of the people eat these animals, but we let it go. He also said that the Spanish with whom they sometimes trade have a name for it, *armadillo*, which means a little armored one. It is a good name . . . it is much like a possum wearing Spanish armor. I see smiles . . . no, it is *true*!

Now, why do I tell you of this? Because later, I wondered if this was a sign that I had overlooked. I do not know, but surely there was a hint there that we should keep our defenses ready. We interpreted it so.

By this time we had encountered villages of Caddoes, and other people who were growers. These people live in grass lodges, made of poles with grass tied on them. Yes, in winter, too. They are not round like the lodges of the Wichitas, which we have seen. These are square. Sometimes there is a big long meeting lodge . . . well, like the Mandans' meeting lodge, but grass. We wondered about the danger of fire, and they said yes, sometimes it happens. This seems not to worry them much.

We were fortunate enough to find a small band of buffalo near one of these towns, and we killed a couple of them for fresh meat. What we did not need, we gave to the growers, which pleased them greatly. That was a fortunate thing all around, because they treated us well, and gave us beans and corn to carry with us. More important, word then went ahead of us that we were friendly and could hunt buffalo well. All through the country of the Caddoes, we were welcomed. This helped us to trade for supplies, and was so successful that it seemed that the sun was shining on our quest.

We pushed on, going almost straight south, a little west. Each time we needed it, there was game. Each time we were in an area where water seemed scarce, it would rain a little. These rains seemed to come from the northwest, as they do at home during this season. But at home, as someone noted, these would be bringing sleet or snow by this time. This made us feel that our quest was good.

One night we were camped in an oak thicket, a pleasant place not near a village, and our watchers heard and saw a small band of animals approaching in the moonlight. They made strange snorting noises, but were the size of dogs or maybe small deer. The horses seemed alarmed at the strange scent, and one of the scouts smelled them, too. He was afraid, because he thought maybe these creatures acted and smelled like bears.

They woke Caddo Talker, who knew quickly what they were. Not bears, and good to eat, he said. They were probably coming to eat the acorns under the trees where we were. Quietly, the watchers woke the rest.

These were strange creatures . . . we killed two with arrows and the rest ran away. I must tell a little more of them, though. They were animals with legs and hooves like deer, but short-necked like bears. Instead of fur they were covered with short bristles. On the back of each one, above the tail, was a musk-smelling opening like a navel on the wrong side. We laughed. The creatures were dangerous, though. As they scattered when we began to shoot, Dog's Leg had the misfortune to get in front of one. It gashed the calf of his leg deeply with its tusks as it passed him.

Caddo Talker called them *pecari*, which is a name that some of the local tribes use for this creature. And, as he said, the meat was very good. He said that the *pecari* seemed much like an animal that the Spanish raise for food.

We took all this to be a good sign, in spite of the injury to Dog's Leg. It was clean, and healed well. It seemed no more than the accidents on any hunt.

Not quite so easy to dismiss was a thing that happened a few days later. We had come to a river, which had low and swampy areas along its banks at some places. Even so, it was pleasant. There were groves of fine nut trees along its course, the day was sunny, and our hearts were good about our quest. We had noticed that many trees—some were oaks of kinds unknown to us—many had leaves that were still green. At home, it must by now be nearing the Moon of Long Nights. So, we thought that this was all favorable.

There was a village nearby, of a hunter-nation who used hand-signs well. They often wintered here, they said. The river was filled with clams, of an excellent size and type for eating, and they use them in part for their winter food. We tried some of the clams, and found them good. Many times later we would have welcomed such food.

These people, who used the hand-sign for "snake" to describe themselves, were friendly enough. We did not mention our quest for a Never-Winter Place to them. We thought that they would fear our entry into their territory. So, we assured them that we were only passing through.

But the trouble, there . . . Lean Antelope was wading in the stream when a snake struck him. He had seen it, he said, but thought nothing of it. It was black and had no rattles, and he ignored it, thinking that it was of the harmless sort we see at home. Even when it struck him, a glancing blow with one fang, he was not concerned. But the pain was unexpectedly severe, and he looked down at his leg. There was the wound, a hole oozing purplish blood.

The skin around it was turning blue and swelling. Antelope staggered up the bank and fell.

It was fortunate that we were with the snake-people, because they knew what to do. Their holy man quickly made a gash across the wound and sucked it clean, much as some do for the bite of the real-snake. And, the bite *is* much the same, their holy man told me. He bandaged it with a poultice. Even so, Antelope hovered near death for three days, while the swelling crept up his leg. It nearly reached his groin, which I thought would be fatal, but then the poultice and the chants and dances, my own and those of the other holy man, suddenly worked, and the swelling began to go down.

Maybe this should have been a warning, too, but we saw it only as a sign for caution. And, we had learned to fear and respect this snake that was new to us, as dangerous as the real-snake. More, maybe, because he gives no warning.

Our friends who helped Antelope called this snake the "cotton-mouth" because of his white jaws.

4

So, my brothers and sisters, we continued on after Antelope had recovered sufficiently from the bite of the snake. It was a few days. The people who camped near had been very helpful, and we had a great buffalo hunt before we left. We killed several buffalo, and of course, gave our hosts most of the meat. They were good horsemen, and we traded weapons, even a few horses.

We talked of turning back there. Some said that we had discovered a fine place to winter if we chose. On the other hand, we did not want to encroach on the territory of a group who had treated us so well. We still did not wish to discuss openly with them all of our purposes, so we did ask where other wintering places in the area might be.

On the last day before our departure, their medicine man took me to the cliff that sheltered them from the north. This was a thing which made it a good wintering place. It was of reddish stone, maybe as high as ten men above the river's level, and about two bowshots from the river. This rocky face lay parallel to the river, for as far as we could see, in both directions. We could see that it served as protection for the winter camp, sheltering the lodges from the north wind. Did I say that theirs were skin lodges, much like ours? It was good to find a people with customs we understood.

But, back to the cliff . . . The holy man showed me marvelous paintings, pictures like we sometimes paint on skins. Well, like our Story Skins. And some of these were similar. One seemed to tell the story of a hunt and a count of the kills. They were painted in red and yellow and black. There were some that seemed to show the sun and the moon, and others animals, birds, and even insects. I could feel the power of the medicine here.

"Is this the medicine of your people?" I asked my friend.

"Some of it. Not all. Some, we think, is very old. See this one, with the crooked lines, like sticks?"

"Yes, what are those?"

"I do not know. They are old. We have been told that the crooked line is a weapon of a type no longer used here."

I was astonished at this.

"But by whom?"

The other man shrugged.

"A people from the south, long ago. Some say they *threw* these sticks. I think maybe they were used to throw something else . . . you know, as a bow throws an arrow."

"*Aiee!* I wonder why this weapon is no longer used?"

He shrugged again. "The people who used them are no longer here. Maybe they found a better weapon anyway."

Yet another question came to me.

"How is it that these paintings are not weathered away? The old ones look as good as your newer ones."

"Yes. I once thought that the old ones knew of some special secret to use in their paint. But I have decided not. The cliff shelters the paintings, as it shelters our lodges, from the north wind and rain. Also, there is some overhang at the top, there. So, they last a long time. Their paint was probably like ours. Pigment, water, a little fat to hold it. Is it the same with yours?"

"Yes," I answered. "My brother, my heart is full, that you would show me these things. I can feel that their medicine is powerful."

He shrugged again. "I knew that you, a holy man, would understand and respect it. It is not my medicine, but that of others before. I have treasured it, and my heart, too, is lifted by its power."

We began to walk back toward the lodges.

"It is said that you leave tomorrow. Your man with the snakebite is doing well."

"Yes, thanks to your skill."

"It is nothing." He waved me aside. "Now where will you go? Home to your Sacred Hills that you told of?"

"I do not know," I told him. "We will talk of it tonight. Our signs have been good for this journey south, except the snake. And since Antelope lived, I am made to think that was a warning, not a sign of trouble. It taught us of a danger we did not know."

Now, this holy man was too polite to question further, so we just visited as we walked.

"How far south have you been?" I asked him.

"Not far. Of course, the river leads to the sea. I went there, once. It is salty, you know."

"So we have heard. How many sleeps?"

"Oh, only a few," he said. "You have good horses, and travel well. But, it is southeast, not south."

Now, when we held our council that night, I mentioned this. That was probably a mistake, because several wanted immediately to go and see it, taste it for ourselves. And I thought it might be good, too. Things were still going well, and there was much excitement. Even Lean Antelope argued to go on to the sea before we turned back. So, Blue Jay decided: We would go on. And, it *seemed* good.

It was farther, of course, than we thought. Is it not usually so? But we did reach the salty-water-sea. *Aiee*, my friends, there is no way to describe it. There is a wild beauty there, and such a great expanse . . . the water reaches Earth's rim! All the soil for a while before we reached the water was not dirt, but sand. White sand. It looked very poor for growing, and few plants grew in it. I supposed, because it was salty. We could smell the saltiness in the air, and that is hard to describe, too. A moist smell, like the smell of a great river, but different. I had not really thought that humans could smell salt, though of course animals do.

Well, we were so pleased to have reached this place that we acted like children, running and playing in the water, swimming out a little way. That was hard, because waves kept coming in, one after another after another. There was a noise, like a slow beat of a great drum, when the waves crashed onto the hard-packed sand. Or, a great heartbeat, maybe. It was easy to believe that the sea was *alive*.

The horses seemed excited, too. They cantered playfully

in the edge of the water, and rolled on the sand of the beach. We stripped and spent the rest of the day swimming, riding, and racing on the fine level beach. The water was warm and tasted very salty. It was a big joke when we realized that with all this water, we had none to drink. We had to take waterskins back inland to a stream we had passed to bring fresh water.

The men who went for water took all the horses to water them, too. We had decided to camp on the beach. Those of us who stayed at the ocean gathered wood and built a fire. There was plenty of driftwood along the beach. There were also many interesting things. Shells of all shapes and sizes, and a few dead sea-creatures that were like none we had ever seen. One, a hand's span across, had a hard shell, and pincers like those of the crayfish that live here in our streams. We learned later that these are good to eat. Another looked like a horse's foot, and had a long sharp stick for a tail.

It was nearly dark when Crow, who was far along the beach to the west, gave a great shout and beckoned to the rest of us. We ran to help him, picking up our weapons, for he seemed frightened. As it happened, he was not in danger, but had only made a strange find. There were the remains of a huge fish, nearly three paces long. It was mostly rotted away, or eaten by the many gulls that we saw everywhere, but we could see its form. What was most amazing was the head. The mouth was large, and all around the opening were pointed teeth, slanted backwards. Each looked like a white flint arrow point, and as sharp. That mouth would have been big enough to put an arm or leg into. The thought made my skin cold, because anything that was encircled by those backward-pointed teeth would not come back out, but be drawn on *in*.

Aiee, it was a strange feeling to see a great hunting fish that was large enough to kill something the size of a dog or a deer for its food. Or a man. We did no more swimming.

We started back along the beach, and while we had been laughing before, everyone was pretty quiet. We arrived at the fire about the same time as the four who had gone for water. They were astonished at our description of the fish with teeth, and they wanted to see it, but nobody was eager to go back there in the dark, because this was country we did not know, and we had already found that there were unknown dangers.

We were quiet that night, after our noisy arrival. Everyone seemed to be thinking to himself. Oh, there was some talk, a few jokes. We commented on the beauty of the stars as they came out over the water. But we were quiet.

There were yet a few more surprises that night. When it was dark enough, we began to notice the colors of the fire. It was not just a usual fire, but of many colors. Now, as you know, there are woods which burn with a different-colored flame. Willow is not quite like walnut or oak. But I am not talking about different shades of yellow and red. There were greens and blues and purples in all the hues you might imagine. It was like a sunset, when Sun Boy adorns himself to cross to Earth's other side.

We discussed this a long time. It seemed to us to be a reminder that the spirits, the medicine, of this place were foreign to us. Still we did not see it as a warning, but as a caution. Later, we wondered if it had been a warning.

Another thing . . . those who went for water noticed when they returned that the water's edge was not where it had been. We watched it for a while, and put sticks in the sand to mark the highest reach of each wave. Some waves came farther than others, but it was true, the sea was reaching toward us. After the finding of the tooth-fish, we were uneasy anyway. Was the ocean angry, somehow, at our arrival? We had lighted the ceremonial fire to announce our presence: "Here we camp tonight," as is proper. But the fire, of course, had not been normal, as I have told you. Were there strange and unknown spirits who were angry? Had we somehow broken some taboo of this strange region?

We stayed close together, and moved our things to a place a little farther from the water, while we watched it advance. No one thought of sleeping.

Then, we heard a coyote call somewhere among the dunes. It made us all feel better, the familiar sound from home. This we took as a good sign, and sure enough: Soon we noticed that the sea was not reaching as high. It was retreating! We laughed and began to relax, and our hearts were good. We still were not thinking of sleep, but there was not the concern that we had felt a little while ago. We learned later that the ocean does this twice each day, and that it had nothing to do with us.

Now, we sat around the bright-colored medicine-fire and talked of home and of what we should do now. We commented on the marvelous things that this day had shown us, and what tales we would tell. . . . We were completely relaxed, happy, pleased at our accomplishment in reaching the sea. We even talked that the beautiful colors of our campfire might be a sign that we had done well, a sign of welcome.

Those thoughts seemed to disappear quite suddenly. There was a gasp from Antelope, and he reached for his bow. We all looked around, and there, standing on a low dune, almost out of the reach of the firelight, stood a warrior. He carried a bow, and he was nearly naked. There were painted designs on his face, chest, and arms. All this we were able to see in an instant, and then he was gone, his form melting into the dunes in the dim starlight. Caddo Talker called out to him, but there was no answer. There was quiet, except for the throb of the ocean's waves on the beach below us.

No one was anxious to search in the dark for an armed warrior in his own country. We built up the fire and waited until morning. We posted no wolves. Everybody was awake and watching, and there was no sleep.

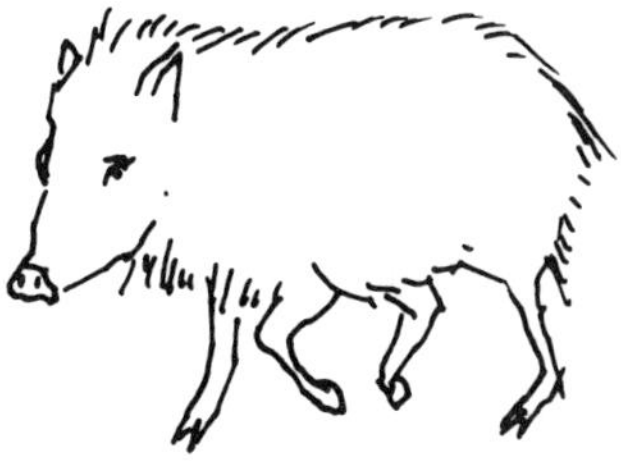

5

It was fully light when we saw three men approaching along the beach. They paused, maybe a hundred paces away, and stood waiting. The man in the middle raised his right hand, palm forward, in greeting. I am made to think that men everywhere do this as a sign of peace. Maybe not . . . I do not know. But even those we met who do not know the hand-signs understood this. Well, mostly . . . but let me go on.

Blue Jay, Caddo Talker, and I went to greet them. They were of a tribe not quite like the Caddoes we had seen, but similar. They knew the tongue that Caddo Talker used, so we could speak together.

They had noticed our fire, they said, after darkness fell, and a couple of scouts had gone to see what it meant. They, too, had had no desire to meet strangers in the dark, so had waited until morning to contact us. Their village was some distance east along the coast.

We gave them a few gifts, and they invited us to visit them. After some discussion, we decided that there was no harm in a day's delay before we started home. We broke camp and followed them.

Their lodges were much like the grass-thatched homes of the Caddoes we had seen. These, also, are growers, but they also catch some fish to use, and like most growers, hunt a little. The buffalo do not seem to come very near their area, staying more in the grassland. But, there are deer that live in the thin brush and timber just beyond the dunes.

We traded a little with them, told stories of our ways, and they of theirs. They seem to have more contact with the Spanish than we had thought. There, we saw many metal knives and tools.

We were gathered in their grass longhouse for this visit, because even there, the mornings are chilly at that time of year. One of their leaders asked about the purpose of our journey, and we explained that we had started in a search for an easier winter camp. I think now that in the excitement of the new things we had seen and done, we had almost forgotten that. Now, we had to admit, we were involved mostly in the pleasure of new sights and sounds, in having fun. It does not make my heart good to remember that. We should have turned back then and started home.

We intended to do that, but there was the constant wonder at what new thing we might see each day. And, the feeling that we all had now that we were on a medicine quest. Oh, yes, we talked with these people of the big tooth-fish. They laughed at us and our fear of swimming because of it. Very seldom, they said, is anyone eaten by these fish while he is swimming.

"*Aiee*," we said, "is not once too many?"

"But we hear," one of their old men answered, "that in your country there are great bears which eat men."

"Real-bears?" asked Blue Jay. "It is true that there are bears who walk on their hind legs and are larger than a man. We do not kill them, for they are much like humans. But the nation of our brother here, who is translating, eats them."

There was a gasp from the assembled people.

"But very seldom," protested Caddo Talker, translating also for us, "is anyone eaten by a bear."

Everyone laughed, we too.

"Each of us has his own dangers," observed an old man, whom I had noticed before. He seemed to be a sort of elder or holy man of these people.

"Yes," I agreed. "It is important to know the spirits of the place where one lives."

He smiled, and I was sure that our spirits met, and that we understood each other.

We told of Lean Antelope's bite from the snake, and how it had happened because of lack of knowledge of the area. The holy man nodded.

"It is the same. There are dangers everywhere, and one has only to learn what they are . . . to understand their spirit."

This was a very wise old man, and I would have enjoyed a longer talk with him. But it was clumsy, the translation through Caddo Talker, and boring to the others, so we gave it up. That was a mistake. He might have been able to tell us of some of the dangers we would face.

Finally, we returned to talking of our purpose, which we found hard to explain. Though we did not realize it yet, probably no one had any clear idea of what we were doing. We were having fun, and convincing ourselves that there was something very important in what we now saw as our quest.

Blue Jay inquired about where the beach led, in each direction. Their answers were vague, mostly based on "east" and "west," which we could easily see anyway. Finally we managed to understand that in some places the coastline is irregular, with many small islands and long strips of sand, separated from the mainland part by little strips of water. In other places, the beach is open to the sea.

Then, they said, there are also rivers which empty into the sea. Far to the east, many sleeps, is a great river not easily crossed, even in boats. I wondered, and still think that this may be the mouth of the Big River that runs to the east of our country. But I do not know. Distances are too great.

Anyway, we then spoke of the area to the west. It is much the same, they told us, except that there is no great river, only smaller ones. They can be crossed without going too far upstream.

"How far?" Blue Jay wanted to know.

"How far upstream?"

"No. How far does this coast reach?"

They became even more vague now. These seem to be people who do not travel much. Of course, they are growers, and stay where they plant. We learned that the coastline begins to bend southwest, and gradually straight south.

"How far?" Blue Jay wanted to know again. "How far south can one travel?"

Again, the vagueness. Again these were people who were trying to be helpful. I had the feeling that if they knew they would tell us, and if they did not, they would tell us anyway.

Then a young woman spoke up. She had lived where we

asked of, she said. There were looks of disapproval, but seeing that we were interested, she pushed ahead. She told of great forests and constant daily rainfall, bright-colored birds and flowers that hang from the trees. She seemed to speak the Caddo language poorly, but Caddo Talker was good—a very good translator. He may have misunderstood some things, but was very helpful.

Then Blue Jay reentered the conversation.

"Can you take us there?" he asked.

This led to great confusion. It seems that this woman was not of this people, the village of our hosts. She had lived in the strange country she was telling about. We were not sure whether she had been sold or stolen or had run away, but she had been married for a short while to one of the men of this village. Then he was killed in an accident of some sort . . . we were not sure what they were telling us.

There was an argument now about this young woman and whether she could leave. One man seemed to have a claim of some sort on her. He became very angry. I do not know . . . we did not inquire too deeply into their customs about women. As you know, there is much difference some-times. Not all women may speak in council, or own property, or vote, as ours do. About these, we did not know. The man who was angry may have owned her, or been a relative of her dead husband. Maybe he just objected to her speaking out as she did. But, we were made to think that here was a woman who wanted to go home to her own people. She really had nothing here. No husband, no children.

Finally, after they argued a while, one of the leaders told Caddo Talker that the woman could go with us if we would give some gifts to the man who was angry. The woman looked at us with her large, sad eyes, and we talked among ourselves. Everyone wanted to help her, and it was not entirely that she was a very pretty woman. We really wished to help her in her unhappy situation. We looked for things that might be desirable to the man who seemed to own her, and came up with an assortment of things to trade. We carried some small things . . . beads and ornaments, things like that, but we had used most of them. Besides, remember that these people have more contact with the Spanish than we do. Our offering met only with scorn.

Then, I realized that they would have little contact with *French* goods. We did not have much, but I did have a metal fire-starter, for striking sparks from a stone. I had traded with our brother Strong Bow for it after he was with the Pawnees, his wife's people. They trade with the French. . . . But you know all this. I remembered that the French fire-starter has a different shape than Spanish or English. I showed it to them, and struck a few sparks from a good piece of blue-gray flint from the Sacred Hills. It may have been mostly the quality of the flint, but I got some good sparks, and they were quite impressed.

I offered the striker in addition to the things we had assembled. The man was hesitant. I finally realized that he kept looking at my chunk of gray flint. Most of theirs are white or yellowish, sometimes pink. When I saw this I, pretending to be reluctant, offered to add the flint into the bargain. He considered a moment, then nodded, and the trade was done.

We were still not certain what we were buying, whether the man owned her or we were paying a debt for her. I thought that we should make sure. Maybe we were just buying her for the night. I inquired of this through Caddo Talker, and we were assured that now no one had any claim at all. She could go anywhere she wished with complete freedom. The man, no longer angry, made motions as if washing his hands. It would be easy, I thought, for these people to learn hand-signs. They almost do it already.

It was in this way that White Flower came to us as our companion. I made a resolve that we should teach her hand-signs as soon as possible so that we could talk together.

Now, I am sure that some of our party were interested in this woman because she was beautiful of face and body, and for no other reason. All of us were attracted to her physically. It could not be otherwise. But mostly, I still contend that we had a feeling that we did this not for that reason, but to help her. Proof of this is that she quickly became as a daughter to us. No, more like a sister.

One thing we were slow to realize, though. This woman wanted to go home. Her offer had originally been to take us south to her homeland. *Hers*, not ours. In buying her, or whatever it was that we did, we were committing ourselves more than we realized. We were accepting *her* suggestions. This was a woman who was already having a powerful influence on our quest.

So, it was in that way that we decided without deciding . . . without even talking of it. Our trail led south.

6

White Flower proved to be an excellent companion. She was cheerful and very smart, and rapidly learned hand-signs. She loved to joke and tease, and anyone who tried to harm her while she was with us would have had to fight us all.

We were never very certain just how it came to be that she had been with the grass-lodge people on the coast. Soon it did not seem to matter. She was especially attentive to Blue Jay, because, of course, he was the leader of our party and made the decisions. She developed a special relationship with me, also, though. She did not flirt with me as with some of the others. I was a little older, of course, but I think she saw that I was a holy man, and looked to me as she might to a father, her special protector. I do not apologize, my friends, for any of us in our wish to help and protect this young woman. She needed our help, and *aiee*, before it was over, she helped us many times . . . *saved* us. But we knew from the first that her wish was to go home. It merely fit well with our mission. At least, we had convinced ourselves so.

Is it not odd, looking back, how we can see that our actions are not really rational? We sometimes wish so strongly for something to be that we can convince ourselves that it *is*. But I will go on.

Flower told us that in the place that was home to her people, it was, truly, never cold. In fact, we had difficulty explaining to her what we meant. When we tried to tell of ice and snow, she was completely confused. She refused to believe that water could become hard, like a stone, or mealy, like ground corn.

"If you can do that," she told me, her eyes filled with mischief, "your medicine is more powerful than I think it is, even."

This, of course, was spoken in the Caddo tongue, and our translator was interpreting. But the young woman was very good with language. Before long she was understanding many of *our* words and using them. Some have this gift, but others will never learn it.

Now let me pause to tell you . . . *aiee*, there is so much! All of the trees there keep their leaves on all winter . . . well, because there *is* no winter. White Flower said that her people knew only two seasons, wet and dry, and she seemed to have no words for "winter" and "summer." We tried to ask her which was wet and which dry, but this was very difficult. Finally, knowing that this was winter at home, I asked whether *now* is wet or dry.

"Dry, of course. The rains come in the other season," she told us.

As nearly as we could tell, the rains would seem to stop at about our Moon of Falling Leaves, and start again maybe in the Moon of Grass-growing or maybe the Moon of Roses. It is hard to tell. But she also told us that the weather is not so much dependent on north or south as on *up* or *down*. That made no sense to us, but finally Gray Hawk remembered the stories of *his* mother, who was of the Mountain band. She always complained of summer's heat, he said, assuring the family that *her* band was in a cooler place during the heat of the Red Moon, because they summer in the mountains. In a *higher* place. Ah, Hawk is gone, now. . . . Forgive me . . . I should not speak the name of the dead. . . . Is there another by that name? Yes . . . the Northern band? It is good. I will try not to make that mistake again. It is unworthy of my gift and my office. But let me continue.

Remember, it was now winter, the Moon of Long Nights, approaching the Moon of Snows. Yet as I have said, we were swimming comfortably in the sea, and not even shivering. At least, until after we found the tooth-fish. Then we stopped swimming *and* shivered a little. But that was not from the cold.

I have mentioned some strange animals and plants, and we were to see even more. But there, at the sea, were already more strange things, before we drew near Flower's forest home with its monsters and bad spirits.

Trees . . . we have many sorts here in the Sacred Hills, and even more in the forests to the east. The willows, elms, all the sorts of oaks, nut trees of different kinds. But there, and on into the hot-land rain forests we saw a tree unknown to us here. There were many sorts, of different heights and shapes, but all had this in common: There were no branches, only a trunk and a single bunch of leaves at the top. No, do not laugh! It is true. These leaves are sometimes as long as I am tall, and shaped like a great fern leaf. Well, no matter . . . it *is* true.

When we remarked on this, White Flower laughed at us. There are even more trees of this kind farther south, she told us, and other kinds, too. She told us of trees whose leaves are so big that they are used to give shelter from the sun or rain, like a robe. Of course we laughed at that, but found later that it is true. The same tree provides great bunches of fruit, yellow and sweet, tasting much like our *pawpaw* . . . but I am getting ahead of my story again!

Anyway, Flower told us of strange things to be seen, things which helped to convince us to go on. Strange animals, hard for her to tell us of with the language problem that we had. She seemed to be describing a creature with no mouth, just a tongue, which ate only ants. But when we asked how big a creature, she indicated the size of a large dog, and with a heavy mane like a horse. Naturally, we knew that she was lying. No animal that size could live on ants alone, could it? But, we told her of the animal that we had seen which rolled itself into a bony ball, the possum-in-armor. She was quite familiar with it, as well as the possum, and it was she who told us its Spanish name: *armadillo*, "little armored one."

Oh, yes, she also knew some of the sea-creatures. The one like a horse's foot, she said, is dangerous! It can sting with that sharp tail. We were glad we had let it alone.

Flower told us much of her land and its beauty. Many kinds of birds, she said, all brightly feathered, live among giant trees. She told of these by names in her own tongue, which meant nothing to us, of course. The whole thing sounded to me like a lie. No, more like someone who is far from home and longs for the sights and sounds familiar from childhood. It is bigger and better in the recalling than it really was in truth. Maybe such a memory is not a lie. . . .

Anyway, one of the things of which she told was the "Smoking Mountain." I felt that I understood the name, for have I not, on many mornings, seen the fog bank roll across a ridge in the Sacred Hills to spill over into the valley? The hills appear to be smoking, no? I was not troubled by her description, but some, taking her description to be real, laughed and questioned her truthfulness.

Flower assured them that the mountain does indeed belch smoke, real smoke, with heat and fire. She became very angry at their doubts, insisting that the hot coals which spill out of the mountain cause fires, sometimes some distance away.

It was in this way that we knew she was lying, and I was sad about it. She could not be trusted. I had wanted to rely on her guidance, but could not now believe it to be reliable.

There was another thing that we continued to notice. The days were still getting not much shorter. It seemed that there would be no Moon of Long Nights.

I asked White Flower about this, as best I could with our constant language problem. It was part of the thing of only two seasons, I supposed, though I did not understand it. I still do not. But White Flower said yes, that nights do become a little bit longer at that time, but they never paid much attention to it. There seemed no reason for her to lie about this, and she was not insistent and angry, so we took it for truth. We were still searching, you see, for the

Never-Winter Place. But like many things that we desire, it was like ashes in our mouths when we—but let me go on with the story.

A little bit more about the woman, White Flower. It is very hard for us, with the respect that we have for our women, to realize that in some tribes and nations it is not so. Even among some of our allies . . . The Head Splitters, for instance, are a little more harsh and demanding. Of course, our women are prettier than theirs, so this may be a reason. Remember, though, the old stories of how the Head Splitters used to raid us and steal our girls for wives, before the alliance? Or, maybe our women are prettier *because* they have been respected and their hearts are good. I do not know.

Anyway, it seemed that this woman, White Flower, came from a people who had little regard for a woman. She had never been treated as an equal! Of course, she had been a captive in some way, at least, with the grass-lodge people on the coast, and her lot was hard. She responded very quickly to us, though. It was a long time later that I began to realize why. She must have expected to be beaten and made to do more than her share of the work. She seemed amazed when we expected her to do only her share. So, she was a happy companion.

Flower also seemed to think that we would all expect to bed with her. She would have been willing, I think, in return for this chance to return home. Some of the men did sleep with her, but she seemed surprised at that, too. She was approached with gentleness and respect, not with a demand. She spoke of it to me, later. Would you believe that among her people women do not even vote in council?

Somewhere along the coast, as we started on . . . about the time it began to turn south, maybe, I noticed yet

58

another strange thing. The Real-star, which never moves, still hung in the northern sky, but it *had* moved. I spent a great deal of time watching it, trying to see what it was doing. The Real-star was *lower* in the sky. I was alarmed when I first realized this, thinking that maybe it was setting, as the sun, moon, and stars do in the west. I did not wish to alarm the others with guessing what might happen. If the Real-star, which never moves, sank below Earth's rim, would the world end? I was confused.

I watched the sky most of one night and found that the Seven Hunters did move as they always had. . . . Their nightly hunt around their lodges at the Real-star was unchanged. The other stars, too, seemed unaffected, and I felt somewhat better. I realized later that the farther south we went, the lower the Real-star hung. I do not know the meaning of this.

All of this, however, reminded me that I had not asked for any guidance for some time. That morning at dawn, I spread the skin on the level sand of the beach and cast the bones. I cannot tell the details, of course, of how a holy man reads the bones. That is handed down from the older holy man to the apprentice. But I can tell you that the objects behaved very strangely. When I shook the cup and rolled them out on the painted designs of the skin, they did not skitter and bounce as usual. Those objects made of stone fell heavily instead of rolling very far across the skin. Bone, and even wooden fetishes which should have told me much, seemed lifeless that morning. I performed the ceremony twice, and it was the same. It was hard to interpret.

I had just finished the second cast, and was not very happy about it, when Blue Jay approached. He was unhappy because his bow had no life in it. He had risen early to try to hunt a little, but had missed an easy shot at a small deer when his bow was not responsive.

What was wrong? Had the spirits of this place rejected us? We talked of it, and both of us were uneasy. Then the sun rose, and we saw a fog bank lying offshore. We laughed about it . . . the dampness of the night had softened Jay's bowstring, and it would dry during the daytime. This could have happened at home.

I said nothing to him about the lack of success in casting the bones. I was trying to convince myself that the skin upon which I cast them had drawn moisture from the fog. In truth, it *had*.

But I was also trying to tell myself that that ominous-looking fog bank out there had no significance. I must have been wrong.

7

What is that, someone asked? The horses? Ah, yes, I did not tell that yet? *Aiee,* there were so many troubles, that was but one. I nearly forgot that. Maybe I am losing my mind.

Well, I mentioned of the damp feel of the air as we moved southward, no? And how the fetishes did not act properly when I cast the bones? I had begun to think that the spirit of the seacoast did not blend well with ours, you see. Part of it was the horses. They were not doing well. They were growing thin and weak.

You know how a horse must spend at least half his time

eating, to stay in good flesh. Not like the buffalo, who can gulp their food quickly, with not much chewing, and then move on to a safer place to chew it later, while they rest. Since a horse cannot do this, he must eat. For a while we thought that we were trying to travel too much . . . too long each day. The horses had been in good shape, and had enjoyed romping in the sea and sand when we reached it. If we reduced our travel each day and tried to find good grazing for them when we stopped, they should fatten again.

We tried this, stopping well before dark each night. It was hard sometimes to find good grass, but the horses seemed to rally for a little while. Then, they seemed to begin falling off again. It was hard to explain. . . . They were listless and weak, and their eyes lost their brightness, the "look of eagles" that we love in our horses. Finally we stopped and camped for several days to wait for our horses to recover. Most of them improved, though very slowly. Two or three, though, made no gain, and continued to lose weight and strength.

We were camped beside a little grassy plain that stretched toward the mountains inland. There was a small stream of good sweet water that ran into the sea here. It was altogether a pleasant place, and one where horses should thrive. But, as I said, some did not. Gray Hawk's mare was, I think, bitten by a real-snake. Or maybe one like the one that bit Antelope, a real-snake without rattles. Whatever, the mare nearly died, her leg greatly swollen and unusable. We tried hot soaks and incisions to drain the poisons. It was apparent that if she ever recovered the use of the foot, it would be a long time.

This led us to take a serious look at our situation again.

There were two other animals that were very thin, too weak to really travel.

As we discussed all this, White Flower suddenly asked Caddo Talker what we spoke about. He explained to her, and she talked with him at length, gesturing with her hands as she did so. He listened and then translated for us.

"The woman says it is not a good country for horses. They sicken easily."

"Ask her more," suggested Blue Jay.

Caddo Talker did so, and turned to us again.

"Many things bite horses, she says."

"The snake? There are real-snakes at home."

"No, no. Other things. Mosquitos, flies."

"Those, too, we have at home," Jay persisted.

"I only tell what she says," answered Caddo Talker. "She tells me that horses sicken and die. Like those."

He pointed to Dog's Leg's horse, which was one of the weak and listless ones. The woman nodded vigorously.

"I am made to think," I suggested, "that this is another thing of the spirit. The spirit of our grasslands is good for horses. Maybe this is not. Or maybe, this spirit is not good for *these* horses. Their spirits do not blend well with those here."

I had examined the horses carefully and found nothing that really showed any cause for the listlessness and lack of eating. It may have been some unfamiliar plant that they had eaten, or possibly the bite of a strange insect unknown to us, as the woman said. I do not know. But it was strange. We could do very little, though I tried some of my songs and spells. And we could not go on or back with three of our horses unfit.

Then an idea occurred to me. This was Flower's country.

What would her people do in this situation? I suggested that Caddo Talker ask her, and he relayed the question.

White Flower shrugged. "Nothing. They will get well or die. Wait and see."

There was much protest at this, and unwillingness to sit and do nothing. Somebody suggested that if we turned back but let the woman go on alone, we would be short only two horses. Two could ride double. This suggestion was quickly hooted down. We already had some loyalty to White Flower, but mostly, I think, the unacceptable suggestion of riding double was rejected.

Then Flower spoke again, to Caddo Talker. He questioned her a little and turned to us.

"She says, why not leave the horses here to recover, and go on, afoot?"

Now the discussion really boiled up. There was the old saying that "a man on foot is no man at all," and of course it was quoted angrily.

Someone else suggested that those with unsound horses stay there to look after their recovery while the rest went on. Blue Jay flatly refused to split the party, which I thought was proper. That decision, of course, cut down the possibilities considerably. We could wait here to see what happened to the horses, or go on, either on foot or with limited horse transportation. Or go back.

It was probably White Flower who decided again. She was very persuasive. I do not mean that she argued or pleaded or any of the other things she might have done. She only made quiet observations, or stated facts. But she had a way of making someone *want* to help her. We felt privileged, somehow, for being *allowed* to do so. Not that she seemed helpless, of course. She was far from that.

Anyway, Flower pointed out that horses do not do well in

her country. Why not leave them here, where they would have grass and water, and the unsound ones could have time to recover while we went a little farther south. Then, we could pick them up on the return trip.

"How far south?" asked Blue Jay. There was something vague about this plan.

But Flower shrugged off the question.

"She says, as far as you wish," interpreted Caddo Talker. "She says, you are the leader."

It is very hard to resist flattery from a beautiful woman, and Jay was only human. The problem was now placed very cleverly back in his lap, but with a good feeling in his heart for the woman.

"Well, why not?" he asked us. "We gain nothing by sitting here while the horses heal. We could start home without them, but it would seem better to recover them later. So, let us go a little way with our sister Flower, here, as she suggests. What is the harm?"

By this time, everyone was becoming enthusiastic. It was as if each one in the party wanted to do as the woman said. And strangely, somehow, each now seemed convinced that this was his own idea. Some people, I have noticed, have this skill, to cause others to come to their side in a discussion without seeming to do so. Even I thought that I had reasoned it out and decided that this was best.

No, it was not an evil influence, a spell that we were under, nothing like that. . . . No one can *make* another think as he wishes. He can only make them *want* to. And White Flower was very skillful at this. We wanted to help her, because we loved her, and because the plan seemed good for us, too, and because by this time, we thought that we had thought of it. It seemed so simple and logical now. We would explore a little, take Flower nearer her home, and enjoy the walk on the beach while we waited for the horses to heal. Of course, we did not know how far it was, or how far she wanted us to go. We had not noticed how vague she was about it.

Thinking back, maybe she did not know, either. To reach her own people, her home, was a tremendous task. She did not try to deceive us. She only saw that we were a help to her as she made her way south. A few days, or many, it would have been good either way. She was going home, and any help that was available was good and was appreciated. She did not intend to put us into all the dangers that later came to us.

I know, I seem to be defending this woman. That may be, and I am not sure why it is. I think that maybe it was this way: We were led to treat her as we would want strangers to treat a woman of the People in such a case. Is that not a good thing? Anyway, I have told you of our thoughts on it, and you must know that our hearts were good. We cannot ask, what if we had done so and so, or not done it. It was done, and is behind us now.

The next morning we started south again, traveling along the sandy shore on foot. It was not as bad as we thought to walk instead of riding. It was a great help that the sand was soft and yielding where it was wet by the waves. We could walk comfortably in the edge of the water, or on hard-packed damp sand a little higher on the beach. Too high, though, the sand was loose and walking was hard. But we tried different ways. Actually, we were much like children at play with a new toy. We were having fun.

Sometimes we would come to a rocky outcrop which made a barrier to our progress. We might be able to climb over it to level beach beyond. But sometimes White Flower would study it and lead us inland. She either knew this country or knew similar formations well enough to lead us where we should go. She was very skillful, a good guide, and her help was appreciated.

It was the same when we came to streams that entered the sea. We allowed her to choose how far inland we must go to cross, and her judgment was good.

I was always glad to get back to the sea after a day of such diversion, though. The land was interesting, but I am not a lover of forests and rocky hills. I am not really a lover of the sea, either, but it is open. One can see a distance, as we can here at home.

Maybe that part was not so bad. The endless strip of white sand, with the sea on our left and the strange land on our right. The feel of water and sand between our toes as we walked . . . We learned quickly to remove our moccasins and carry them. . . .

The nights when the moon shone were beautiful. It was something like a full moon over our Sacred Hills. Not so beautiful, of course, but if you had never had the advantages of living in the grassland, you would think it good.

Looking back, though, I now see that strip of sand as a deception. It was pleasant and tempting to follow that white and easy trail. We were deceived. We thought it led to more interesting sights, more knowledge and experience. And in truth, it did.

We did not understand at the time, though, that it led to danger and death.

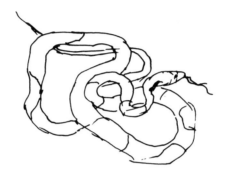

8

As I tell this, it is easy for you to see where we were wrong. I admit it. But at the time we were in an exciting adventure. From time to time I was uneasy, to be sure, but I know that the others were, too.

We were coming to an area where we saw a flat, open plain at times, with areas of thick forest between. Inland to the west were mountains, sometimes close, sometimes farther. Sometimes, even, we could not see them for a day or two because of dense timbered forests. We noticed that the mountains seemed dry, while the air was more moist on the coast. After the problems with our bowstrings and with my casting of the bones, we realized this. We moved inland, but the traveling was so much easier at the sea that we kept returning to the beach.

We held a council there one evening. We must decide how far to go. A fire burned brightly in all the colors that still puzzled us. ("That is the way it is with sea wood," White Flower had told us.) Behind us, heavy growth of forest came fairly close to us at this point, and we knew that the mountains lay beyond. Everyone was uneasy, because the sounds and smells of the night are so very different there. Its spirit is different. We could feel the night's dampness creeping in on us, and it was quite uncomfortable. Remember, though, it was very pleasant in the day, and at that time you were all huddled in your lodges to keep from freezing!

I mentioned night sounds . . . some were much like ours. . . . The call of the coyote. *Aiee*, Coyote is everywhere, I think. That was comforting, a spirit we understood.

But there were also other sounds that were not very comforting. One was like the cry of a great cat, like the cougar. We wondered if it was the same, and tried to ask White Flower. That was difficult. Maybe the hardest things to understand in another's tongue are animals and birds, for they all have their own names. With a great deal of difficulty, then, we used hand-signs and Caddo-talk and some of our own words to try to inquire about that scream in the night. You know how the cougar sounds . . . like a woman being tortured. This was worse, maybe.

After several false starts, we were able to understand that "cat" was right. Then, to our surprise, Flower said, through Caddo Talker, that it was a spotted cat. Now our spotted cat, the short-tailed bobcat, is never bigger than a dog, though very fierce. We know his cry, not nearly so loud or deep.

We looked at each other in surprise. The cry we had heard came from a much larger beast, maybe bigger than a cougar. I was thinking to myself that if their bobcats are bigger than cougars, *what must their cougars be?* It was not a comforting thought. I could see the whites of many of our eyes around the circle, and we all edged closer to the fire.

But then, White Flower laughed at us. "It is only a lonesome cat out in the trees," she teased.

Maybe this was like a challenge to our manhood. No one wanted to admit that he had more fear than this slim woman. If she, who knew this country, had no fears, why should we? Later, I realized that it was much like the tooth-fish for those grass-lodge people, or the real-bears for us. A danger, but one that is not great to those who know how to avoid it. White Flower, you remember, was near the fire, too. She also would scorn the danger because she wanted to go home.

We started the council, with Blue Jay leading. The sea was calm and beautiful, the sand smooth, and a half-moon was riding high, to faintly light the beach. The Real-star hung low in the north to remind us that we were far from home.

Blue Jay asked for comments, and several spoke. I do not use their names for the reasons we spoke of earlier, except when I know that another bears the name, too. *Aiee*, it still hurts, my friends!

"How far shall we go?" asked Blue Jay.

He was the organizer and leader of the party, and we knew that he was brave and full of courage and would want to continue. That was part of our problem, of course. No one wished to seem less than brave to his leader, and Jay's feelings on the subject were well-known. I had already decided to remain neutral. I could best fill my responsibilities if I did not take sides.

There was silence for a little while.

"How far would *you* go, my brother?" asked Caddo Talker.

Now, again, see how it was with this man, a Head Splitter. They are our allies, have been for generations. But they have a fierce and fearless reputation to uphold. Would Caddo Talker wish to turn back? No, he would go on as long as any of us wanted to. The opposite was also true. We thought that night of home, of warm lodges banked with snow against Cold Maker, and of warm buffalo sleeping-robes and warm wives. No one wanted to be the one to suggest turning back, however.

"I would want to see a *little* farther," said one cautiously.

"I, too."

"It could do no harm," said a third.

"Whatever you others want," yet another said.

No one, you see, wanted to be the one. . . . I am made to think that Blue Jay knew this and planned this council to happen just this way. Is he not a wise leader? And I wish with you that he will recover quickly.

We talked a little longer, and then Blue Jay spoke. "It is good! We go a little farther."

White Flower, who could grasp enough of the conversation to know the decision, clapped her hands like a little child. She was, in truth, a child in many ways, though she must have seen and suffered much in her short life. Her pleasure in our decision made us feel good, of course, good that we had chosen wisely. It was not so, of course, but we did not know that, then.

We asked Flower more about the country ahead, and of how far it might be to her people. Many sleeps, she said, which seemed strange to us. We had thought that surely we were nearing the place that would be the farthest we could go. She laughed at that. But what would stop us? we wondered. Another sea?

"If there is water on our left and land on our right, what stops us?" asked one man.

"We are walking around a big salty lake," guessed another. "We will come back to the place we found the tooth-fish!"

Flower laughed at all of this.

"It makes no difference!" she insisted. "But no one has ever been as far south as he can go. Except maybe the Old Ones."

I was interested in that. I have always longed to know the secrets of the Old Ones, whose lodges and towns are scattered through the mountains west of our country. Some of our people, you remember, once took refuge in one of those cliff ruins on a trip to Santa Fe to trade for metal knives.

But Flower, when we explained this, said that no, these were different Old Ones. The ancient people she spoke of, who lived before *her* people, built great cities, lodges taller than the greatest of trees in the forest behind us, placed on hills that they made for the purpose.

"Greater than anything the Spanish have," she insisted.

"Greater than Santa Fe?" someone asked, laughing.

"I do not know this *Sennafay*," she stormed, "but greater than anything *you* will ever see!"

It was amusing, and they laughed a lot and teased her, knowing that she lied.

We had seen some people along the coast, small clusters of mud lodges with roofs of grass or of leaves of the trees I spoke of, the ones with no branches. These leaves are tough and spiny, like the yucca soap plant here, and make a good roof, if one can stand such a dwelling. We slept outside when we stopped with them.

These people used narrow boats like the canoes of the French who visit our Eastern band. But these are made of a log, hollowed out, instead of the bark canoe. Heavy? No, no . . . they are scraped very thin. They paddle these out in the ocean a little way, and then throw a big net, braided together from plant-fiber cords. It is pretty to see them throw these . . . like a great butterfly, fluttering over the water. Oh, the purpose? To catch fish! We were invited to go out with them, but no one went. We were still thinking of the tooth-fish. . . .

A few days after we had the council on the beach, we met some people of a different sort. We had completely stopped trying to leave the sea to travel, because the forest was becoming more and more dense and tangled here, with fewer open spaces.

It happened this way. We were walking along the shore, keeping watch on the dark jungle beside us. *Aiee*, sometimes I became lonely for the open tallgrass country here, where you can see all the edges of Earth. I felt sometimes that the forest was closing in on me, crowding me into the sea.

There are many sounds that such a forest speaks in daylight, too. The cry of birds, the scream or call of animals somewhere in the tangle of vines and underbrush. These are not so fearsome in daylight, of course, but worrisome enough. In that dark thicket there could be many creatures, only a few paces away, watching us, unseen. It was like the feeling when a hunter feels he is being watched as he stalks a deer on a rocky hillside and then discovers a cougar above him. The hunter has become the hunted in the space of a heartbeat. It was like that.

There was a sudden gasp from the man in the lead, and I turned to look. I had been looking toward the sea, trying to stretch my eyes to relieve the strain of looking at that wall of green on my right. I quickly turned, and there, stepping into the light from the dark forest was a man. He was maybe twenty steps away. He was tall, well-built, and carried what appeared to be two long spears. One had no point, and it seemed to me that he carried this rod carefully, as if it had great importance to him. The thought crossed my mind that maybe he was a holy man, and that this was his medicine stick.

Most impressive, maybe, was his robe or cape. He was naked, except for a breech-clout, but tossed over his shoulder and tied at his side was a magnificent spotted robe with short silky hair. It was from a large animal, gold with black flower-spots on it. It did not take long to reason that this was Flower's "spotted cat" of the forest, the screamer who sounds like a dying woman. We learned later that this was true, and its name was *jaguar*.

White Flower shouted something to us, a warning in her own tongue, but there was no time to translate. As we learned later, she had tried to tell us to stand still and make no sudden moves. But, it was too late. One of our impulsive young men raised his bow, probably only to threaten. The jaguar-man, almost calmly, raised the rod that he carried and put the end of it to his mouth. The other end he pointed at us, and I saw something leap from it. It was quick, my friends, like the flick of a frog's tongue at a moth, and the moth is no longer there. You thought you saw a brief flicker . . . it was like that.

There was a gurgling sound at my elbow, and I turned to look at the warrior who had raised his bow. His eyes were wide and staring with surprise and fright. He seemed to be trying to speak, but could not. And there on his neck, just above the bony notch here in the center, there had appeared a little puff of fur . . . downy fluff, like the soft breath-feathers of *kookooskoos*, the owl. This furry ball was sticking there, as if it had sprouted and was growing. The unfortunate young man dropped his bow and clawed at the thing with both hands as he sank to the sand, still making those horrible gurgling sounds. He pulled loose some of the downy stuff, but it was no use. In a very short time, he was dead.

White Flower was yelling, and for a moment I thought that our party would try to kill the stranger. That would have been a mistake. I had seen that we were up against something we did not understand, a very powerful weapon. I tried to stop our young men.

"Wait!" I yelled. "Stand still. Do nothing until we understand this."

At about the same time, Caddo Talker and Flower managed to establish talk, and he called out much the same thing. The weapon, you see, was a tube through which the jaguar-warrior *blew* a short, slender arrow feathered with this downy stuff.

It was good that our party did nothing more to attack the man or we might have all been killed on the spot.

Because now, other warriors were slipping out of the jungle to surround us. Each wore the spotted skin of the great cat, and I realized why. In the mottled shade of the dark forest, they had been practically invisible. Each carried a spear, and some carried the blowguns.

They must have been watching us for some time, I thought, and my friends, my heart was not good about this. Their leader motioned for us to lay down our weapons, and we had no choice but to do so. They moved into a semicircle around us, penning us against the sea.

9

We lay there in the dark hut, listening to the chanting and the drums, certain that this was our last night of life. We had been separated from White Flower, who was much concerned over all this. Her worry did nothing to make us more confident, either, as you might well expect.

They did not tie us, as they seemed to think we would not try to go into the dark jungle unarmed. This in itself discouraged such thoughts. So did the thought of the great spotted cats, a matter of great concern. We had not heard any that night, but that proved nothing. We did, however, hear another creature, one we could not identify. It made a frightening roar, not like the cat's scream, but a deep bellow, like the challenge of a buffalo bull at rutting time. The grandfather of all bulls, maybe. But deeper . . . it is hard to describe.

So, we huddled together as darkness fell, and tried to make ourselves inconspicuous. They did place a guard at the door with a blowgun. There was not much urge to try to escape.

This was a village of many lodges, built of mud like those we had seen, and thatched with the leaves I spoke of. But this was a country that seemed to have much more rain, and we wondered if the mud of the lodges would not wash away. We were not thinking of that then, of course. We were too frightened. We learned later that they use a mixture of sand, mud, and ashes to plaster their lodges . . . well, no matter. . . . This is the part that still fills me with dread. . . . No, I must tell you anyway . . . listen!

When we left the beach to go to the village, two men stayed behind to strip the corpse of our fallen brother and, we supposed, to take his scalp. But shortly after we were placed as prisoners in the mud lodge, one of the men gasped and pointed out the doorway. The two men who had remained at the beach were bringing the body of our brother. They had tied his hands and feet, and hung him on a pole, as we would sometimes carry a deer, between two men. This was a terrible thing to see in itself, but the worst was to come.

We could not see well, but they seemed to be hanging the corpse by the feet. We did not want to get too close to the door where the guard stood. The light was poor as night drew near, and we could see only that several men clustered around the hanging body. Finally, one of our young men managed to see what they were doing.

"*Aiee!*" he cried. "They are *skinning him!*"

It was true. We took turns, standing in the small corner from which we could see. It was dreadful to watch, but we were compelled to do so, fascinated by this bizarre ritual. We talked of singing the Song of Mourning for him, but were afraid to draw attention to ourselves.

When they had finished their grisly task, flaying our fallen warrior like an animal, one of their men stepped forward and the others draped the bloody skin over his back. We could not believe such a thing. They tied the skin in place at wrists and ankles, and we finally realized what they were doing. This would be a reenactment, a dance in which the man wearing the skin would portray an enemy. Yes, that was it.

The dance went on and on, other dancers with spears pretending to jab at the "enemy." Some blew a puff through the tube of their blowguns, pretending to shoot the deadly little darts. Our hearts were very heavy for our brother, and of course we were wondering about our own fate.

We had not been badly treated so far, beaten only a little with slender sticks. But we were very uncomfortable. It was hot and muggy and the mosquitos were fierce, their bites like the sting of bees. We also wondered what small creatures might lurk in the dark corners of the hut. They have scorpions there a hand's breadth long.

We were sitting there glumly, and I was trying not to guess at what ritual might be reserved for us. Blue Jay was watching out the door and gave a gasp that caught our attention. One of the others shouldered forward, took one look, and staggered backward. I thought for a moment that he had been struck with one of the blowgun darts, but it was only shock and horror that thrust him backward. I ventured to look. To my surprise, the jaguar-men were cutting pieces of flesh from the corpse and *roasting* them on sticks over the fire.

One of our young men turned away, sought a corner, and vomited. We had eaten nothing, so he had little to vomit, but I felt much the same myself. Were we to be saved for *food* by these people? Fattened, perhaps, like dogs fattened for eating? It was not a pleasant prospect.

Yes, my friends, we actually did watch these people eat strips of flesh that had been part of our brother. One of our number could not stand it any longer.

"I am leaving," he stated, his voice trembling. "The guard is not watching well."

"But, the jungle creatures—" I began, but he interrupted me.

"I will take my chances with the spotted cat," he said angrily, "before I become food for these men."

He waited until the guard was absorbed in watching the grisly feast, and then slipped out, around the corner of the wall and into the darkness.

"I go with him," said another impulsively.

He, too, slipped out, but this time the guard was alert. Whirling, the jaguar-man raised his blowgun and we heard the soft sound, a deadly puff as its dart leaped forward. Apparently it missed in the darkness. The guard came back, glanced inside, and growled something to himself before he settled back at his place.

Aiee, it was a long night, my friends. We slept little, of course. The celebration finally quieted and people drifted away. Oh, yes . . . at the climax of their celebration, they threw the skin and what remained of the body into the fire and built a great pile of logs over it. The flames reached high, and swarms of sparks flew upward.

It was then that we did sing the Mourning Song for our brother, to help his spirit find its way to the Other Side. The guard looked around, but said nothing. We did not care . . . we had by this time given ourselves up for dead.

Some time after things quieted down, we heard the scream. It may have been the cry of the great cat, but I thought not. I still think not. There was a human quality about it, and I think it was the death scream of one of our brothers. We never knew what happened to the other, or which one . . . but I am getting ahead of my story again.

When morning came, a different guard appeared, an evil-looking man with his teeth filed to points. I had noticed this on one of the others when we were first captured, but did not realize its significance. It made my flesh crawl to look at him.

A woman came to offer us a bowl of some mushy substance, but none of us tasted it. We had no appetite for it or for the day ahead of us. Fasting, I thought, brings the spirit closer to the spirit-world. Surely we were close already.

I was wondering also what had become of White Flower. Was this not her country? Or maybe these people were her enemies. She might be kept as a slave, and be no better off . . . even worse, maybe, than she had been with the grass-lodge people. Anyway, my heart went out to her. She had tried to help us, even though it was to help herself. She admitted that. And now, both had failed. She had not been able to return to her people, and our mission, the lofty goal of exploration to the Never-Winter Place, was ashes in our mouths. Our families would never know what had happened to us. Our bones . . . our *ashes* would nourish not the grassland of our ancestors, but this strange forest with its strange spirits. Our flesh . . . I did not want to think of it.

It was about midmorning when four heavily armed warriors came to the hut and spoke to the guard. He stood aside and the one who appeared to be the leader of the four motioned us outside. We went. It was better to go standing tall like men than to cower before our captors. We intended to die with courage, to show the dignity of the People. We had talked it over and had decided. When Blue Jay gave the signal, we would all attack our captors and die fighting. The signal would be the war cry of the People, the deep, full-throated battle cry that had struck fear into our enemies for many generations. Blue Jay had agreed that he would resort to that only as a last effort, when they seemed about to harm any one of us. We could not let them kill us one at a time. So we were ready. I had picked the man I would attack . . . grab his knife, get too close for him to use his spear. . . . Yes, we would take some spirits with us to the Other Side.

Now we were approaching a larger lodge, which seemed to be a meeting place. There were many people there, and our escort guard motioned us inside. A man who appeared to be a leader sat on a little platform at one end, and there was a space before him. We were herded forward to stand before this leader and his subchiefs.

Then I saw something that made my blood run cold. On the floor near these men sat White Flower. She was clean and unhurt, and her hair was combed and pulled back as she always kept it. She was plainly not a prisoner.

This, maybe, was the greatest hurt of all. After all we had endured, after we had worried about the fate of this woman we had all come to love, was it possible she had betrayed us?

I could think of no other explanation. There she sat, unafraid, and though she looked worried, she *should* be, I thought. My anger rose, and I saw the others also react.

"What is she doing here?" asked Blue Jay. "She has betrayed us!"

I thought for a moment that he was about to rush forward to try to kill her. But there was something here that we did not understand. We should know more before we acted.

"Wait," I said. "Let us learn more of this. You can kill her later."

But my heart was very heavy. The only thing that I could think, too, was that we had been betrayed. Why? What did she have to gain by sacrificing us? Finally, an answer came to me. We knew nothing at all about White Flower's people. This must be her nation, or one of its towns. Yes . . . *her* mission was now a success. Flower was home. These were *her* people, and for her, it was over. For us, too, in a far less desirable way. I would have thought she would show gratitude, but she had let us be taken prisoner, one of us killed and eaten, two more probably lost. My rage grew. I turned to Caddo Talker.

"Ask her," I demanded, "are these *her people?*"

The leader on the raised platform looked straight at me and voiced a single word. I did not know any of his tongue, but I could easily understand his meaning.

"Silence!"

At the same time, one of the jaguar-men whacked me sharply above the ear with the shaft of his spear. I staggered but did not fall. His intention was not to kill me or even knock me down, but only to discipline.

I was silent.

10

▼▼

N ow, my friends, of what I am about to recount, I want you to know that I did not understand all of the conversation. It was carried on with difficulty, with both White Flower and Caddo Talker interpreting as they were able. So I tell you not what I heard and understood, but the ideas that were exchanged. I was still dizzy from the blow that I had received. My head was aching and a knot the size of a duck's egg was rising above my right ear. Much of this was told to me later.

Now the crowd quieted, and the leader started to speak. He was a handsome man, wearing the jaguar skin that was now so familiar. He also wore a headdress of feathers, beautiful shiny green, which come from a bird that lives in their jungles. There were also feathers of red, yellow, and blue, bright and shining. These other colors were for trimming . . . the main one was the shiny green.

Now, this splendidly dressed man spoke, but not to us.

"I thought there were ten?" he asked.

"Yes, two ran away into the night," he was told.

"Ah! Too bad! Which one talks to the woman?"

"That one," said a warrior, pointing to Caddo Talker.

White Flower tried to speak, but the leader waved her down and turned to Caddo Talker.

"You speak her tongue?" he asked.

Since the man spoke his own language, Caddo Talker had no idea what he said and could not reply. Finally the leader turned angrily to White Flower.

"My chief," she protested, "I have tried to tell you, he speaks the tongue of the Caddoes, which I have also learned. He does not know yours, nor do I know his."

It appeared to anger the leader that he must talk to us through a woman, but it seemed the only way.

"Ask him what they do here," he snapped.

White Flower started to speak, but reconsidered and made the requested inquiry. Caddo Talker explained that he was not of our nation, but had come along with us to assist in communication.

"But you do not speak our tongue," the chief observed.

"That is true. But the woman does. She speaks the tongue of a people to the north, the Caddoes, and I speak the same, though not well."

Again, there was complicated explanation, through both interpreters. The chief seemed still not certain of the situation, which was understandable. By that time none of us was certain of anything. It occurred to me, though, that if we were to be killed and eaten, our captors would not go to the trouble to talk to us. Does one converse with the beans that will go into his soup, or the puppy being fattened for the kill? No, I was made to think there was something more here, which I did not understand.

When all the different people who were involved got things sorted out so that they could talk, it worked this way: Our captors knew the nation of White Flower's people, though they looked down on them. These were not her people, and she had not betrayed us at all. But she was a woman, and of a nation they considered inferior. They hated to talk only through her. They had to, of course, because no one else knew our captors' language at all.

Then she would translate for Caddo Talker, and he for us. It was very clumsy, as you can imagine, and made things quite slow. The jaguar-chief demanded to know why we were so far from our own country, and we tried to tell him of our quest, the search for a place to winter at first, and how we had then wondered how far south it is possible to go. It all sounded very childish and unreasonable to us as we tried to tell it, but to my great surprise, the chief nodded.

"I have sometimes wondered that myself," he said. "You have no other reason?"

We assured him that we did not, and he then inquired more of Caddo Talker. It seemed hard for him to understand why one not of our tribe was with us.

"Your nation is not theirs, then?" he asked repeatedly.

"No, but we are allies, brothers for many lifetimes," Caddo Talker explained. "I came with them because I could talk to Caddoes for them, and because I, too, wondered about the south."

The chief nodded. "And what of you?" he demanded of White Flower.

Flower knew his tongue well enough to answer directly.

"I am going home. These men helped me."

He seemed to think about this for a little while, and then nodded, but as if he had a little doubt.

We still had many unanswered questions. Seeing that the chief had come to a pause in his questioning, Blue Jay began to demand some answers of our own. I was hoping that he would not push too hard. If we angered this chief, he could have us all killed instantly, and this was not a comforting thought.

"Ask him," Jay demanded, "why his warriors killed, skinned, and ate one of us."

Possibly Caddo Talker toned down the demand a little, and maybe Flower did too. For whatever reason, the jaguar-man's answer was quite mild.

"Ah, yes! We honored him as a brave man."

When this answer came back, Blue Jay became filled with rage.

"It is no great honor to be skinned and eaten!" he yelled.

Some of us tried to restrain him, while the chief sat with an odd puzzled look on his face. Flower relayed the answer and the man spread his hands in consternation, talking to her earnestly. She conferred with Caddo Talker, who turned back to Blue Jay.

"Yes, it is!" he explained. "This I do not understand, but he says that they have given their highest honor to our brother. To eat of the flesh of a brave man is to honor him and his bravery. He is surprised that we do not know that."

Caddo Talker shrugged helplessly, unable to explain further.

Blue Jay responded slowly, but at least he was not so

angry that he might endanger us. Finally he calmed enough to make a reply.

"Tell the chief," he said reluctantly, "that we are honored." Then he turned, and spoke aside to the rest of us. "But I hope we are not honored any more. One can take only a little honor of this kind."

Caddo Talker relayed his reply, the first part of it, and the chief nodded agreeably. We still had the concern as to what would be done with us. I think that in the minds of us all there was a question: If this was how they *honored* someone, what would be done with those who deserve *less* honor? There was a second question which came to me, and probably to some of the others. What would be done with White Flower? It was apparent that these people had little regard for her, and that she was being used for her ability to translate.

Apparently Caddo Talker had the same concerns that I did, for he later told me of this conversation with the chief, relayed as I have told you. They had agreed to release us, but wished to keep the woman. "Because she has some value," the chief said. "That will repay us for our trouble."

Without even consulting the rest of us, Caddo Talker boldly began an argument. He knew that these people seemed to have little regard for *her* wishes, so he cleverly assumed their attitude.

"It is true, my chief, the woman has slight value. But, we have bought and paid for her, though only a little bit, and she is ours. We needed her to translate, as she does now. It would be very difficult for us to travel and trade without her talking skill."

I do not know, of course, how accurately Flower translated this. Caddo Talker did not know, either. But she was a clever woman, and it is surely true that she played the situation to her own best interests . . . that is, with us. She might still be a captive, a slave-wife with the jaguar-people, if Caddo Talker had not argued for her.

The chief shook his head, displeased. It was apparent that he had been struck by her beauty, too, and wished to keep her. He motioned with a gesture that even I could tell was a command to go. It was at that point that Caddo Talker boldly stepped forward, planting himself in front of the woman.

"No!" he said firmly. "The woman is ours!"

For a moment I thought that we were all dead men. The warriors in their spotted skins stepped forward, spears ready. Remember, we were still unarmed. Our weapons had been taken from us on the beach. I was imagining that Caddo Talker would be struck down in an instant. I was ready to do as we had agreed, fight to the death rather than be slaughtered like fattened dogs.

There was only the space of a heartbeat before I would have struck out at the man on my left, but a strange thing happened. The chief stopped the warriors with a gesture of his hand. And, though it seems a miracle, he was *laughing*.

"You are a brave man," he said through our interpreter, "even though you see what happens to brave men. Are all of you this brave?"

Now, Caddo Talker was faced with a real problem. He could say yes, we were all brave, and possibly cause us to be flayed and eaten. Or, he could deny it to try to save us by declaring us cowards. We did not know all of this, of course, only that we were threatened and ready to fight. Caddo Talker managed to keep his calm. He turned and looked at us, waiting there to see what would happen. He could not claim us cowards, he said later, even if it meant the death of us all. He turned back to the chief.

"Look at them, my chief," he said. "Do they look like cowards? They are ready to see how many of your young men they can take with them when they cross over. How many are you prepared to lose?"

It was a bold bluff, and the chief appeared to consider for a moment. We were waiting, and it seemed like a long time. White Flower crouched there, also waiting, her face pale, eyes wide with fear . . . no, not fear. Worry, maybe. I only saw her show fear once, and that was later. But forgive me. My spirit is weary. I will try to stick to the story. . . .

The chief glared at Caddo Talker.

"Do not threaten me!" he cautioned. "I have only to lift my hand!"

"It is not a threat, my chief. I only tell it as it is."

It was probably good that none of us others understood what was going on. We would have probably started the fight that would leave us dead in that mud hut.

Finally the chief smiled, a smile with his mouth but not with his eyes.

"It is tempting," he said through Flower. "It might be amusing to watch such a slaughter. But enough! Go, and take the woman. You have been enough nuisance already."

I did not understand this, of course, but I saw White Flower's face relax and break into a smile, and it was good.

"Now," continued the chief, "let us see what we can find of your men who ran away."

Everyone began to relax. Our weapons were brought and returned to us with much ceremony.

"Let no one make a move," cautioned Blue Jay. "This is still very touchy."

They even brought the weapons of our dead brother, who had been killed with the blowgun. We were unsure what to do about that, but Caddo Talker solved the problem for us. He ceremoniously placed the weapons before the chief.

"So that your people can remember the honor of a brave man," he explained.

It was good that we did not understand what was being said. I doubt that any of the rest of us could have been that calm. Caddo Talker, with less personal attachment than that of the People, was able to do it. It was good that he was with us, for it probably saved all our lives.

HESSTON PUBLIC LIBRARY
110 E. SMITH
P.O. BOX 640
HESSTON, KANSAS 67062

11

It may sound strange to say that from that time, we were on rather friendly terms with the jaguar-people. But we were.

We went back to the lodge where we had been held, and tried to track the departing steps of those who fled into the night. Snake-Road, our tracker, was very good, as you know. He said that this tracking was very different. The marshy ground, rotting plant material underfoot, little sprouts of green everywhere. Sometimes I thought I could *see* things grow, it was so fast. Vines tangled everywhere, and there were bright-colored flowers in the trees.

The whole feeling of this place was damp and steamy, and it all smelled like the river bottom after a flood. Fishy, stinking. Now imagine trying to track in that! As I look back, I can scarcely imagine that we had even gotten ourselves into that situation. But it had seemed right at the time.

Three of the jaguar-warriors had come with us to the hut where we had been held, and one was a tracker. He and Snake-Road worked together. They picked up a track where the two of our party had slipped around the corner of the hut and into the tangle of the forest. It was hard to see how they had done it, because the paths were hard to follow, even in daylight. They must have simply blundered into one of the game trails that wander through the trees and bushes. You know how a deer trail sometimes squeezes through a dense thicket in a river bottom? It was like that.

We were all following the two trackers, and I for one was marveling at their skill. As I thought about it later, maybe it was not so hard. If the fleeing men had been on this trail, they would *stay* on it, because there was no place to *leave* it.

We came into a little clearing and stopped to let the trackers circle a little, trying to see what they could find. The rest of us waited.

It was a pretty place, if we could forget the tragedy that we dreaded to find. That and the ceremony of the night before, and the stink of the deadly swamp, and . . . Maybe it was not a pretty place at all. But we were alive, the sun was shining. Things did not look quite so hopeless. Near me on a trailing vine was a delicate white flower with a red throat. Birds sang in the trees, birds of such magnificent colors—blue, green, yellow, red, sometimes all on the same bird. I wondered which might be good to eat.

Later, we found that almost anything *can* be eaten, if you are hungry enough.

I think it was there that we also saw lizards of several kinds. Tiny ones that clung to tree trunks or even to the giant leaves of the forest plants. There were larger ones, too, some as long as my arm. These were good to eat. There were snakes, too. . . . But, my story . . .

Pretty soon, the other tracker motioned to Snake-Road, and the two cautiously approached the edge of a swampy sort of pool. It looked muddy and foul, and not the sort of place to drink, or even swim. There were rotting logs floating in the water, and I was made to feel that the spirit of this place was bad . . . evil.

We could not see what the two trackers saw, but they were bending over a muddy spot where there seemed to be a great many flies buzzing. It was on a sort of mud slide, such as otters make in our country. You have seen otters at play, climbing up the bank to slide down a slippery place again and again? This seemed to be like an otter slide, though not so steep. But it *was* slick and muddy.

Then I realized . . . what could attract flies like this but *blood*? They must have found something that was not good news. The two trackers pointed at the spot, then at something a few steps away, and moved in that direction.

About that time, I noticed that one of the floating logs seemed to be drifting toward the bank. It took me a moment to realize that it was only one log that was drifting, and that *there was no current*. Just then White Flower yelled a warning and the trackers jumped back away from the water.

It was good that they did so, because that log had changed itself into a giant lizard. It had been that all along, of course. That is its way. As the snapping turtle of our rivers lies on the bottom pretending to be a rock while he waits for his prey, so did this log-lizard. Only *we* were its prey!

I must describe this creature for you . . . a fearsome thing! It was as long as three or four paces . . . no, really! It is true. About a third of the length was its tail, which can lash from side to side fiercely. A blow from that tail could kill a man. All four legs have claws like a bear's, and the mouth . . . *aiee*, my friends, you have never seen such a thing! The mouth opens, each jaw as long as my arm, and there are many teeth . . . tusks like those of a real-bear, the grizzled bear who walks upright like a man. Now think, though . . . the jaw of this creature is maybe three times as long as that of the real-bear, so there is room for many more teeth.

Flower told us that this is the creature who bellows like a bull in the darkness of the swamps. She also said that few people are usually eaten by these great thunder-lizards. Again, to each nation there are dangers, I suppose. Real-bears, the tooth-fish, and to the people of this swampy forest, the thunder-lizard.

What, then, had happened to our brothers? Apparently in the darkness and in their terror, the two had come down this trail and had blundered into the lair of the great lizard. One was seized, Snake-Road told us . . . that was the bloody spot. This probably explained the scream we had heard. It was the death cry of the one who was dragged into the water. The other escaped, the trackers said. They could see his trail as he ran.

We followed that trail into another of the tunnels in the tangled foliage. We did not, still do not know which of the men survived the thunder-lizard to meet some other end later. And we do not know what ever became of the other man. By noon the trackers had lost the trail and could not find it again. You must realize that it is as I said. Everything is growing so fast . . . vines, plants of all sorts, funguses, mushrooms. The spirit of such a place is evil and oppressive. We could have walked within a step or two of our friend's body and never have known. Maybe we did . . . but we were forced to give up the search.

Now, I was so oppressed by the way the forest kept trying to swallow us that my heart was very heavy. I longed for the Sacred Hills, our tallgrass prairies of far horizons. My eyes ached, and I needed to stretch them. I needed to sit by a fire in front of my lodge and watch my wife broil a feast of fresh buffalo hump-ribs after the fall hunt. I had lost track now of what season it would be at home. The Moon of Hunger? Moon of Awakening? I did not know. It struck me as a grim joke that maybe we had found the Never-Winter Place and it was worse than the winter itself. I felt trapped, closed in by this place of bad spirits, and I was glad when we decided to head straight for the sea again. At least there we could stretch our eyes and see Earth's rim, even though it was water.

We camped that night on the beach, having reached it a while before dark. The jaguar-men left us and we were alone. At least, we could feel the fresh air from the sea, and that was good. The brightly colored fires raised our spirits a little. We pulled ourselves together enough to sing the Song of Mourning for the brothers we had lost. White Flower looked on sympathetically. She understood our grief.

Now, let us look a moment at our situation. We were ten . . . only eight were warriors of the People. Blue Jay, Snake-Road, Antelope, Gray Hawk, Dog's Leg, myself, and two others whose names we cannot speak. Then Caddo

Talker, who had joined us later . . . *aiee*, a good man. And the woman, White Flower. We were three less than a day ago. Our party seemed much smaller and more vulnerable.

As darkness deepened, the night-creatures of the forest began to scream their cries. It was a bad feeling that I had, with all the tragedy that this quest had already caused us. It was a place of bad spirits.

I think others felt it, too, because I noticed as we lay down to sleep that we were closer together than before. Each needed the closeness of another's spirit for comfort. I lay down between Blue Jay and Caddo Talker, all a little way apart. Pretty soon Flower returned from attending to her personal needs and looked around at the reclining forms. Then she seemed to come to a decision. She stepped between me and Caddo Talker, wrapped herself in her robe, and lay down on the sand, her back to me. I moved over a little to give her room.

I understood. She must have had a very hard time. It had been quite possible that we would all be killed and she would have been a captive of those jaguar-people. We had quickly noted the low esteem that they had for women, compared to women among the People. She also knew that her safety was largely the result of Caddo Talker's bold bluff, at no little danger to himself. Next to him, she felt secure. I merely chanced to be on the other side.

We settled in, a little restlessly. Snake-Road was our sentry, and someone else would relieve him later.

I had performed my evening prayer-chant ritual as I always do, though it was difficult to find the proper frame of mind. How can one celebrate the setting of the sun when it happens behind a screen of tall forest, with stinking swamps and dangerous creatures and evil spirits? I felt better after the songs, but not much. I lay a long time listening to the dreadful night sounds and wondering what would happen now.

We had few supplies. We had used most of them as we traveled. As you know, hunting parties or explorers often have to eat their horses to survive, and I thought of this, but we had no horses now. Maybe we could recover some as we retraced our steps, but even that was not sure. We would need to depend on White Flower to tell us how to live in her strange country.

I finally fell asleep, holding in my hand the amulet that hangs around my neck, the elk-dog medicine of the People. It has been a force for good for many generations, and has brought the People through many bad times. Surely it would help us through this country of bad spirits.

12

We were pleased and thankful to be away from the dangers of the people we had encountered there in that steamy, swamplike place. That night we had not even talked of what to do next.

I had assumed that we . . . the survivors . . . would try to make our way home. We had encountered many things, had touched many strange spirits, had been helped by some and hurt by others. Now we must lick our wounds and retreat, no?

Imagine, then, my surprise when we rose next morning and Blue Jay called a council. Surprise not at the council, for that was proper, to plan our return journey. No, I was surprised at the questions that our leader raised. Not those I had expected, but one main point for decision: *What* shall we do now? I think most of us had thought that we would start home. Yet here was our leader, proposing a council to decide whether to continue our southward journey.

I do not wish to make it seem that I questioned Blue Jay's leadership. He had proven himself. But this thing of turning our journey into a quest . . . Of course all of us had done it. Jay perhaps more than the rest. He is a man of vision. The rest of us were willing to follow that vision. Does not that itself prove his leadership? It is seldom that a leader comes along whose followers are so loyal that they will follow him to the death. Running Eagle, our Warrior Sister, was one. . . .

But, forgive me. I only wish to make it plain that though I was surprised at Blue Jay's council that morning, I did not doubt his leadership. He started the discussion with the open question.

"What shall be done now?"

Several of the others must have felt as I did, that we should of course start home. We were quiet, startled that he should consider anything else. Finally Dog's Leg spoke.

"Are we not to start home?"

Blue Jay seemed irritated.

"We are to *decide*," he said crisply.

It was quite plain, then, that he wanted to go on. There flashed through my mind that maybe some bad spirit, some unknown influence of this strange country, was drawing him on. For him, it was *still* a quest. There were things unanswered that his spirit still sought. We all began to see that now.

Now, how could all of us be swayed in our thinking that morning? I cannot answer, except that we were. But think about it. We were ten, counting the woman. She, of course, wished to return to her people. Blue Jay, too, felt drawn southward. There were two, maybe three others, who would do anything that Jay suggested. That made up about half of our little group. Caddo Talker was by this time showing more attraction to White Flower, and I was trying to remain open-minded, befitting my station. That, you see, was most of the party. Who was to argue against that many?

Someone asked again about how far Flower's people might be. Again, she was very vague. I do not think that she was intentionally so, but that she really did not know. She had been carried off, traded, sold. We never learned all the tragic things in her past. But I was made to think that her heart was good. She just did not know the answer to what we asked. Of course, you must remember that she wanted badly to go home. That may have influenced her, made her think that it was closer than it really was. Or maybe she lied, to help her get home. I do not know, and I do not want to know.

Anyway, her encouraging answer had some influence on those who were the most fiercely loyal to Blue Jay, and they began to enter the discussion.

"Why not go on a little?" one asked. "The danger is behind us, and we are alive. Is that not a good sign?"

Everyone had to agree that being alive is, indeed, a good sign. But it brought up the subject of signs. Blue Jay turned to me.

"Walks in the Sun," he began. "Tell us, holy man, what signs *you* see. Can you cast the bones?"

I had been thinking about that ever since the previous attempt. I had been working on an idea. In damp weather at home, the drums do not ring true. It is well-known that the cure is to warm the skin of the drumhead over the fire. I recalled watching and listening to such a ritual, while the skin dried and tightened, creaking in protest from time to time as it tightened against its lacings.

Now, I thought, could life not be brought back to the casting of the bones by the same method? Actually, it was plain that the problem was with the surface on which the objects are rolled. The skin. It had become softened by the water in the air, deadening the bounces and roll of the bones, wooden fetishes and stones that are used in such a ritual.

"I will try," I answered. "But first I must drive out some interfering spirits."

I unwrapped the skin and spread it carefully, knowing that the painted symbols on its surface would also be more fragile. With much thoughtful prayer I held the skin over the fire, letting the warmth drive out the water spirits that had softened it.

Of course I did not expect the tightening and creaking that comes with warming the drumhead. But before long I could tell that the feel of the skin was changing. The limp, soggy texture was becoming firm. Life was returning to this, one of my most important means of forecasting the signs. It was good.

I spread the skin in a level place on the sand and aligned its patterns to the sun and to where I knew the Real-star to be. I had taken care to note its position before dawn. Now I shook the little box with my special indicators and cast them across its surface.

It was a good throw. The little fetishes jumped, bounced, and rolled with new life. The change in the surface had restored the usefulness of the spell. We also learned that warming our bowstrings in the same way restored our weapons, but that is another story.

I now studied the toss, trying not to be hurried. It did not help that everyone was peering over my shoulder. I finally asked them to step back so that I could perform my task. The indicators, you see, were confusing. I cannot reveal, of course, how I am able to interpret such things. It is part of one's apprenticeship to the holy men. But, it is enough to say some of the things I saw.

First, there was danger. We knew that, of course. We had just come through it. Some of the pieces indicated the three deaths we had just experienced. There was a buffalo tooth that suggested that some of us would again hunt or eat their flesh. . . . You know that another holy man might have interpreted these things differently. There were also strange patterns, with many of the little indicators lying *across* the lines, indicating both good and bad, and once more I wondered if my medicine was good here. Was it weakened, with the Real-star so low in the night sky? I did not know. I still do not. There were two other things I noted, though. One was an indication of the importance of a bird fetish. The other, not so important, was a small fetish indicating a man or men. I was uncertain and was not able to give a very good interpretation, or to forecast much. I told them what I could and related the conflicting signs. When I told of the bird sign, Blue Jay became excited.

"Would this not be a sign for me, the Jay?" he demanded.

"Maybe," I admitted. "At home, it would mean to watch for the crow, who is close to the spirit-world. Here, we have no crows."

"Is there another bird here?"

"I do not know," I replied. "Let us ask Flower."

It was done, and she assured us that yes, the bird who wears the shiny green is a messenger.

"But he lives deep in the forest," she added.

We did not like that, and there was much muttering and

shaking of heads. The others disliked the dense forest as much as I did.

"We cannot go plunging into the forest looking for this medicine-bird," argued Dog's Leg.

Others nodded. It was not practical, just to see if he carried a message. Maybe so, maybe not, and could we understand it, if he did? It would be like one of the jaguar-men trying to talk with our crows. Could he understand?

We stood there, not knowing what to do, and suddenly Blue Jay pointed, upward and to the north.

"Look!"

Three birds were sweeping toward us, following the shoreline. They were of a kind that we had seen before, but never this well, and never so significantly. This is a sort of heron, about the size of our great blue heron, the fisherman of our lakes and streams. But this bird is brightly colored. All over, he is a rosy pink, like the sky in a winter sunset, or the bloom of the brightest of roses. No, it is true!

But most amazing is its beak. Not long and pointed like the heron, but rounded. It was rather foolish looking, actually, as if it wore a spoon on its face. Yes, the beak was very like a horn spoon. Well, you may laugh, but it is true.

These rose-colored spoon-bills swept directly over us, three of them, which in itself seems important, the three. Then they veered and took a new course, a tiny bit west of south.

"That is the direction of my home," the woman signed.

"It is good!" shouted Blue Jay. "We are meant to follow White Flower!"

We were immediately caught up in the excitement. It was easy, you see, to follow an exciting leader. It was also a glorious sight to watch those great birds sweep over us and hear the whistle of their wing feathers as they passed. It *was* exciting.

I was pondering the three . . . three *days*? Moons? Maybe just the significance of the number itself, like three crows, who are closer to the spirit-world as messengers than one. Maybe, no significance at all. Sometimes it did seem that we had no rules at all to follow, here. I was to think more on that later. Also, why was there no warning of illness when I cast the bones? Or of the snake?

But I am getting ahead of myself again. Forgive me.

At that time, I *was* pondering one other thing: The hint that we would be in contact with other men. White Flower's people? Maybe, but I thought not. This was something else, something strange and unknown.

13

It was about three sleeps later that we camped at the mouth of a little stream, where it emptied into the sea. It was a little bit early in the evening to stop, but we did not wish to be still looking for a crossing as darkness fell. We usually thought it best to cross and then camp, so as to get a fresh start in the morning, but this night it did not appear there was time. Besides, the early stop would give us a chance to hunt a little, and our supplies were low.

We had scattered some, not the best of actions we might have taken. But the area seemed secure, the forest not too dense or threatening. We scouted a little way into the trees, and found a game trail that led to a watering place at the stream. It was maybe a hundred paces from the beach. We noted that it would be a good place for a bowman to hide and wait for deer or whatever creatures of the sort might come to water at dusk.

"It is good," signed White Flower, "but let me bring water for our use first."

We turned back toward the beach, where Flower picked up the waterskins and went back. Some of the men were picking up driftwood for the fire, up and down the shore. As I have told before, a fire was not as essential for warmth or cooking as it was for a symbol. We were particularly aware that in these places of strange spirits, we should announce our presence. The fire was a declaration: *We are here. Here we stay tonight.* By way of apology to the spirits who dwelled there, we always offered a pinch of tobacco to them each time we stopped for the night.

So, Antelope busied himself with starting the fire, while we gathered fuel and Flower went for water. Later, we would post the hunter at the water hole.

Now we should have sent a man or two with Flower, but there seemed no need. It was quiet. This seemed a safe area. She had assured us that there would be little danger here. And after all, was it not her country? She above all of us should have known. But never can anyone see all the dangers that lie ahead . . . or, just beyond the next step!

I had just tossed an armful of sticks on the pile and paused to watch Antelope. His fire-bow was twirling the spindle in the fire-board, and white smoke was rising in a cottony puff. We had had some problems with starting fires because of the moisture in the air here. We had begun to roast and dry a handful of tinder over our previous fire each morning, and to wrap it tightly . . . but never mind.

Caddo Talker was approaching, carrying more wood, when we heard the scream. This was no spotted cat that sounded like a woman, but a *real* woman's scream. It came from the direction of the water hole, and we knew that White Flower must be in trouble. Caddo Talker dropped his firewood where he stood and sprinted into the forest. I was close behind him, and not until we were well into the tunnellike path did it occur to me that neither of us was armed except for our knives. I heard someone running behind me. I hoped devoutly that whoever it was, he had picked up a bow or a spear.

We burst into the clearing and I saw a dreadfully horrible sight. Near the water's edge lay White Flower, struggling in the coils of a giant snake. It is hard to tell you of my feelings. I stood there with a feeling of helplessness. The body of this creature was as thick as my thigh, here. I could not see how long it might be, because it was wrapped and knotted around the body of our friend. She stopped screaming, because she could no longer draw her breath. The great coils of the monster were drawn tightly around her waist.

You may have seen one of our snakes at home catch a bird or a rat? You know how it will strike and hold the creature with its jaws for a moment until it can slip a coil or two around its prey and crush the life from it? It was that way. This great snake had caught Flower's leg in its jaws between ankle and knee, and even now it was sliding yet another coil around her upper chest and across the throat. It required little imagination to see that this tremendous pressure could not only strangle, but probably crush ribs and even larger bones.

I could do nothing but stand there and watch the brightly mottled loops writhe and tighten. I admit it, my friends, I was afraid. I almost turned to run. Flower's face was the color of ashes, and turning darker as she gasped for her last breath. Her eyes were wide and staring and I thought she was looking at us for help that we could not give. I felt guilty and ashamed.

Just then Caddo Talker, who had stopped as I had, leaped forward and flung himself into the writhing mass of flesh there on the ground. He was screaming the falsetto war cry of his people at the top of his lungs, a chilling sound. He had drawn his knife and slashed at the thick body of the snake. The mottled skin opened in a long gash, revealing quivering muscles beneath.

This only infuriated the creature, however. The jaws loosened from the woman's calf and the head swung . . . it was as broad as my hand. . . . The jaws darted quickly to a new position on the wrist of Caddo Talker. This was the hand that held the knife, you see, so he was defenseless. I should say that the bite of this snake is not poisonous like that of the real-snake. It has many small teeth, meant to *hold* its prey, and well suited to do so.

Now, Caddo Talker too was trapped. He tried to pull away, but the jaws held fast. He struck at the head and at those beady, expressionless eyes with his other hand, but could not free himself. I saw one of the thick mottled loops loosen from the body of White Flower, enough to enclose its second victim also.

Beside me stood one of the others. He held a bow, but it was useless. One could not shoot an arrow into that writhing mass without fear of hitting one of our people.

Terrified as I was, I could not stand there and watch my friends killed. I ran forward, trying to think as I did so. The head . . . it was directing the movements of the body. For some strange reason I remembered the teaching that

126

had been given me as a young warrior: In a battle, try to see who is the leader of the enemy and put *him* down first. This leaves them without a leader, and the battle is half won. I had never had occasion to use this advice, but now it came to me in a flash of memory. My guide was helping me, or I could not have done this thing of which I tell.

I grasped the throat of the snake, as thick as my wrist, and held it tightly while I began to slash at it with my knife. I felt the creature jump and twitch as I cut through layer after layer, through skin and muscle. My blade struck bone, and I despaired for a moment. But the jaws were loosening. I held on tightly, knowing that the head would turn on *me*. One more slash . . . I felt my blade slip between the neck bones and realized that it could cut the spinal cord. I gave a last thrust.

There was no question when it happened. A great convulsion overtook the entire body of the creature. Wild, undirected motion, knocking me aside, tossing and twisting loops that flung us all aimlessly around the muddy bank. The head now flopped loosely on the strip of flesh and skin that remained. Blood gushed from severed vessels and splashed over us all.

I rolled clear and turned to grasp Flower's hand. She was limp as I dragged her free of the writhing coils. Caddo Talker was also struggling free, as the spasmodic activity of the dying snake's body began to slow.

We laid the woman's still form gently on the grass and tried to see if she was alive at all. It seemed a long time before we saw her try to take a breath. Caddo Talker then picked her up to carry her to the beach. The movement seemed to stimulate her, and she opened her eyes about the time we reached the open. It was not quite sunset. I spread a robe on the sand, and Caddo Talker placed her on it. She was beginning to draw big gasps of the air of which she had been deprived.

We all stood anxiously while she recovered consciousness. It had been a very close thing. In a little while her breathing was better, and it began to seem that she might recover. She was still confused, but we knew that we must wait and see.

After some discussion, we decided to try to eat the flesh of the snake. No one wanted to hide alone in the woods to wait for game to come with darkness coming on. Four men returned, and brought meat and waterskins back to the fire.

The meat proved very good, light in color but a bit soft in texture. I have eaten worse. But the whole happening was very disturbing. Once again, we were dealing with strange ways and strange creatures. We had been very fortunate to escape at all. Even so, Caddo Talker's right wrist was torn, from the snake's jaws.

"It is nothing," he insisted.

White Flower's left calf, too, showed the marks of the creature's teeth. There were two sets of bite marks. Apparently it had caught her, started to fling its crushing loops, and then shifted the jaws for a better hold. I shuddered to think of it. Oh, yes. She said that she thought it had dropped from a tree, but was not certain. Her first warning was the jab of pain where the teeth closed on her leg.

We prepared for sleep, still very uneasy. Our wolves . . . we posted two . . . stationed themselves well away from the brushy undergrowth at the edge of the sand.

"Be careful," White Flower advised through Caddo Talker. "Sometimes they come in pairs!"

That was not a comforting thought, either.

We talked long that night, with some disagreement.

"We have escaped this danger," Blue Jay stated triumphantly. "Does that not prove that our medicine is good, our signs favorable?"

I said nothing. Blue Jay had not seen the fight in the clearing by the stream. In fact, he and two others had been some distance down the shore when it happened. By the time they returned, it was over, and the snake was dead. To them, it seemed no great event. They did not know how close to death Flower had been, and possibly Caddo Talker also. To them, it was a fortunate thing to have meat.

I am sure that by now, several would have been more than happy to go home. Yet no one wanted to be the first to say so. I suppose it was a matter of manhood. The woman, too, was a great influence, maybe. When she was so determined, so brave, and showed so little fear of the forest, how could we deny her?

She assured us that the incident with the snake was highly unusual. There were stories among her people of such things, she said. But she had never known firsthand of such an encounter. Her manner was very encouraging.

I noticed one other thing that night. Flower had recovered sufficiently and had learned the full story of the fight, and the part that we had had in it.

"I thank you both," she said in the hand-sign talk that she had learned from us. "You have saved my life."

But somehow, the grateful look that she gave me was not quite as deep or meaningful as the smile that she bestowed on Caddo Talker. If I had been single, I would have felt very elated about a smile like that.

Even as it was, my heart was good.

14

W e camped there another two days to allow for good
recovery of the injured members of our party. By
this time, of course, we were thinking of White
Flower as one of us. When we have camped, eaten, and
faced danger together, there comes a special relationship.
Caddo Talker, too, had become one of us. Though Head
Splitters were always allies, for many generations at least,
this man had become special to us because of his bravery.
And because of the fact that we three had fought the snake
together, we had a special closeness. It was odd, three
people of different nations were now closer than any others

in the party. We were friends, and we trusted each other. We had proven that trust with our lives.

Anyway, we crossed the stream before dark on the evening of our second day there. We would start on early the following morning. We had not seen another of the great snakes, for which we were all thankful. I, for one, would rather face a real-bear, I think. Maybe not. But we did not see the mate of this snake. Maybe it had none and was traveling to search for one.

As we moved on, our pace was a little slower. Even though she was recovering nicely, White Flower walked with a slight limp. The powerful jaws of that snake had bruised the muscles of her leg. And, it was easy to see the many tiny punctures where the teeth had broken skin. We still marveled at the width of the creature's head, easily seen by those rows of tooth marks on her shapely calf.

Caddo Talker walked well, but his right hand was swollen, and the fingers did not yet work properly. He finally determined that it was worse if he swung the arm naturally as he walked. The swelling ran down his arm and puddled in the injured wrist and hand. He protested that it was all right, and I thought it was. He had no sign of redness or swelling, which would indicate a bad spirit in his wound. I noticed finally that he had discovered something that helped. He was hooking the thumb of his injured hand around the thongs that held his backpack around his shoulder. That kept the hand high and the swelling began to recede. It would be good to remember.

We talked of it that night, and I helped him prop the hand up for sleeping, tying it loosely to a tripod of sticks. By morning the hand was considerably improved, and in another day or two it was so much better that he could close it into a fist. I thought it very fortunate that in the damp sweat of this seacoast, neither of those bitten by the snake had more problems. The wounds remained clean and unfestered, and healed quickly. I considered this a good sign.

It was about this time that we saw the large anthills. They were bigger than any we had ever seen, a heap of sand and bits of clay that I thought at first were made by some animal that digs in the ground. Well, I can tell you how this one meadow appeared. It was like a town of prairie dog lodges scattered across the level plain. The mounds were much larger, of course, and I wondered what sort of digging creatures might make these lodges. I was expecting maybe an animal the size of a dog.

But Flower laughed at me, and said no, these were the lodges of ants. I doubted her, and thought she was teasing us, until we went to look closely. It was true. There was no opening to these lodges, except for the small holes where ants went busily in and out. They were very large ants, and it was good not to stand still too long near one of these lodges. Their bite on a bare ankle was quite uncomfortable.

We saw one of these lodges that had been torn apart, as if a bear had clawed it. This made us uneasy, but Flower told us not to worry. I wondered if this might have been done by an animal like the little armored possum, the *armadillo*, but larger. She laughed at me and insisted that no, this was done by the creature with no mouth of which she had told us long ago. Then we all had a good laugh, knowing that there could be no such creature. I decided that the ant-lodge had been destroyed by something like a badger, searching for mice. I doubted that I would ever be really sure.

We had stopped there, near the place of the ant-town, and were preparing to camp on the beach for the night. One of our wolves called softly to come and look. There among the ant-lodges was a strange beast. It was walking along, pausing to scratch at the mounds. It moved rather slowly, and in its way of walking reminded me somewhat of a skunk. But it was as big as a large dog, had a shaggy mane like a horse, back feet like a bear, and front feet with great claws like those of a badger. These it used to claw into the ant-lodges. And oh, yes! A big shaggy tail.

Yes, you laugh! We did, too. There was never such a beast. But I did not even tell you yet of its head. It was very long and slender, half as long as my arm but no thicker. It tapered from the little ears smoothly down to a point no bigger than my finger, and *there was no mouth!* This was the creature that . . .

"See! It is as I told you!" White Flower signed to me in triumph.

We could not believe it, and tried to move closer. Flower assured us that it was harmless unless attacked. We did not intend to attack it, and managed to watch it as it fed. That, too, was as Flower had said. It would tear open an ant-lodge, and while the thousands of ants were scurrying to start defense of their home, this creature stood calmly and flickered its tongue, lapping them up. No, lapping is not right. There is no word for what this beast does. The tongue is sticky, like that of a frog, but long and thin. It traps many ants on that tongue, and then draws them inside through this skin tube that it has instead of a mouth. The hole is hardly bigger than a finger. Yes, I hear your disbelief! I did not believe, either, until I saw it.

I asked Flower what this animal is called. She told me a word, which I did not understand. Her tongue is strange, the words hard to say, with many clicking sounds and flutters of the tongue. Finally she and Caddo Talker discussed at length and he turned again to me. *Ah*, I thought. *Now we will learn about it.*

"She says," Caddo Talker stated simply, "it is called the 'one who eats ants.'"

Everyone howled with laughter, that after such a search in several languages, we would learn something that we could already see for ourselves. I have decided that it is often so. We call things the same as others do, many times. We only use words that sound different.

Oh, yes . . . a couple of our party learned that the anteater is not entirely defenseless. While it cannot bite, and its tongue is harmless, it *can* defend itself. They tried to corner it to examine it more closely. The animal flung itself on its back, making a hissing squeal, and began to slash with those great front claws. It was easy to see that it could do great damage to an attacker. White Flower assured us that even the great spotted jaguar, larger than our cougar, is cautious about these slashing claws. Our warriors withdrew, and the anteater shuffled off into the woods.

It was somewhere in that area that we came also to a town. These people were fishermen and growers. Or at least, harvesters. It was hard to tell. They were friendly, and Flower spoke their tongue. Those who are growers are usually friendly, I think. I decided this is because they *must* be. It would be too easy for an enemy to destroy their crops, so they try not to have enemies. It is different for hunters. They can fight or move on, or maybe both.

Anyway, this village was good, and we stayed there a few days. We hunted some, sharing our kills with our new friends. In turn, they gave us food. Beans, corn, dried squash, and some things unfamiliar to us.

These people lived in the mud houses I spoke of, with

grass or palm-thatch roofs. They also plastered the outside walls with mud mixed with ashes, which seems to keep the mud bricks from washing away in the rains.

This town also seemed to have much contact with the Spanish. They had metal knives and tools. More than we do, really. Some big metal pots that they cooked in, and flat sheets of heavy metal for use in their cooking. They have a thin sort of cake made of ground corn which is cooked on the flat metal. They kept several kinds of birds in cages. Ducks, turkeys, and others, for food and for their eggs. Also, some brightly colored birds, just to look at. But enough of this.

While we were there, it rained. *Aiee*, it rained! This, said Flower, was the beginning of the rainy season. By this time we had lost all sense of what moon it might be at home. I was beginning to think we should be turning back. As it happened, we could not have turned back or forward or in *any* direction while this rain continued. Several days it pounded us, and it was good that we happened to be still at the village, where we could take shelter.

There was hard wind, which threatened to blow the roofs from the lodges. Some of them *did* lose their roofs, and the people struggled to replace them whenever the storm slackened enough.

Most frightening, though, was the sea. *Aiee*, it was like a living thing! You know how a wind will lash our rivers or lakes until every wave is topped by a curl of white? It was like that, except so much bigger. The great waves would start far out in the water, one following the other. They were no longer the beautiful dark blue that we had seen before, but gray. Ugly, ash-colored gray. They rushed toward the land, each taller than a man, and when they came close they would blossom at the top with a white curl.

It would reach landward, overrunning the wave itself, hungry and threatening. Then it would reach the shore, trying to leap out at us, crashing to the sand and slithering back into the sea. It was loud and frightening and we stayed well back from the shore. Most of the time it was raining, so we stayed inside anyway.

We spent time in storytelling and in gambling and playing some of their games and ours. We taught them the plumstone game, using small pebbles we picked up on the beach, and painted red on one side. Also, our game with sticks hidden in the hand. They had similar games, and we exchanged stories. That was interesting, though many of their stories were of animals that we did not know, so they were hard to understand. Ours were the same for them, of course. They knew nothing of some of the animals we told of. They refused to believe in our little owl who digs in the ground, or the rabbit who turns white in winter. We did not even try to tell them that there are birds who do the same, farther north, or of the ermine in the mountains, who becomes white with a black tail. They knew nothing of snow, so how could they understand creatures who change their color to hide unseen in a snowy season?

So, we did not believe all of their stories, nor did they believe all of ours. It did not matter. We were friends, and we passed time pleasantly. One does not have to believe everything he hears. And it is the privilege of a storyteller to stretch a tale, is it not? Stories are made to be told.

It was disappointing, of course, that some of our stories, like that of how Bobcat lost his tail, were useless. It is not the same when the listeners have never seen a bobcat.

15

fter a few days, the rain began to clear a little, and Caddo Talker approached me, with Flower at his side.

"Flower says we should be ready to move," he began. "There should be a little while . . . a few days . . . until the next storm."

"Wait, move where?" I asked.

"That is why we came to you first," he went on. "This is where we turn southwest, away from the coast. The shoreline turns slowly east, and we must go west."

I had noticed that the beach, which is irregular anyway,

143

had been bending to the east for some time as we traveled. I had thought it maybe just a variation, but I was completely unprepared for this suggestion that we leave the coast. In fact, I was thinking in terms of going *back*, not leaving the sea to go inland. The sea, at least, was a landmark that we could not lose. Unless, of course, we left it.

It seemed to me that this was the time to make the decision to turn back. Flower was among people that she knew, if not her own. We had come to no conclusions about the south country, except that it did not seem suitable for buffalo hunters of the tallgrass prairie. In a way, then, we *had* accomplished our purpose. At least, to the extent that we really should go home.

Looking back, we never would have gone so far, would not even have spent that first winter in the south, if it had not been for the woman. She was a powerful person, a leader who could induce people to follow her. That was strange, as I think of it now. It would not be unusual for one of our women of the plains to be so, for it is our tradition. We have had warrior-women, as other plains nations have. But White Flower was of a people whose traditions do not encourage strong women. Maybe her hard life had made her so. But, it was good, and we admired and respected her for it.

Now, however, came a different situation. We would be holding a council to make the decisions as to what we would do. Probably today. But here was an inkling of a split in our group. Caddo Talker had sensed it. Or maybe Flower had felt it, with the keen intuition for such things that women seem to have.

No matter how it started, these two had approached me to join them in a coming political split. I was not comfortable with it. It was not the place of a holy man to take sides in such a council.

"My friends," I said, "I cannot say what we will decide in council. I must not take sides in this."

Caddo Talker translated, and it was plain from their faces that they were disappointed. They did not appear to hold a grudge, and I had to admire them for their open and forthright attempt to enlist my help. I was sure that if the decision went against them, there would be no hard feelings toward me.

As it happened, the council took some very odd turns. Blue Jay opened by asking Flower to tell of the country ahead. Caddo Talker was in the process of telling her of the request when one of the other men spoke angrily.

"Wait!" he cried. "This is madness, Blue Jay. We have lost three men, and we can see that this country is evil for us. We should be planning our return, not thinking of going on!"

The rest of the circle was quiet, waiting. I had not known of Blue Jay's intent to go on, but now I thought more about it. You all know our friend Jay. Since he was small, he has been willing to try things never done before. He is daring. He inspires others. I had thought at one time that he had an interest in the woman, and I think he did. As we all did. Now, it began to come to me. That was not his strongest drive. Maybe, even, the woman was a convenient excuse to do what he wanted to do: to explore farther than any of the People had done before.

Now think, though. He had already done that, and his curiosity was not yet satisfied. His driving force was leading him—and us—yet *further* into the unknown. But it appeared that there was a rebel faction that might split the group in two. Again, I quickly made a mental count.

Flower, Blue Jay, and Caddo Talker would want to go on. Antelope and one other, whose name cannot be said, usually followed Jay without question. Others, whose names do not matter now, were unknown in their opinions. I was trying to remain neutral for the present.

Even though there was much input into this sort of war council, the will of the leader or organizer usually carried great weight. So, there would probably not be enough opposition to sway the decision. And I was unprepared for the violent argument that ensued.

Blue Jay looked coldly at the man who had raised the objection.

"Are you a coward?"

The other man hesitated under Jay's accusing gaze.

"No, but I am not foolish, either."

Blue Jay became enraged at this. I do not want to belittle a brave man who is a great leader. I only try to explain how this happened. It was such a foolish thing on the part of everyone. We knew better than to split the party. Forgive me a moment. . . .

There, now. I will try not to become so tearful. Let me go on. Blue Jay accused the man of making jokes about his family. Jay's grandmother was of the Eastern band, you know, but despite their reputation, many great leaders have come from that band. We all know this as one of our jokes, and no one takes it seriously.

Except that in this case, we were all strung as tight as a drumhead on a dry day. When he heard the word *foolish*, it was too much for Blue Jay. I admit, he has been teased all his life about his kin in the Eastern band and their reputation for foolishness. But I never thought that he was bothered by it. I guess we never know the inner hurt that we give to people with our childish jokes. I never saw Jay react like this.

"You will not speak ill of my grandmother's family," he hissed.

The other man was as surprised as I.

"I never thought of your grandmother," he retorted. "I do not even know her. But I *do* know foolishness when I see it."

He should not have said "foolish" again. Blue Jay was livid.

"You are disloyal!" he shouted. "I should never have let you come with me on this quest."

"And I should have had the good judgment to stay home!" retorted the other. "This was a mistake."

Both had jumped to their feet and I thought they would attack each other. Antelope rose to step between them, but Blue Jay pushed him aside. Jay was quieter now, but his voice was icy as he spoke.

"That is a mistake that you can correct!"

"And so I will," the other man replied, equally cold. "I turn back today. Who goes with me?"

Again, I thought Jay would strike him, but he did not.

"Yes," he said calmly, "who goes with him?"

He looked around the circle. None spoke for a moment, and then another man rose.

"I go with him."

"Wait," I said. "Let us not divide the party. It is too dangerous."

"No more dangerous than following a madman," snapped the other man.

You realize that I am not using the names of those involved. This is for two reasons. First, the taboo about speaking the names of the dead. Some of the names may belong to people who still live, so I could use them. But I do not, because it is not good to make an issue of whose fault it may have been to split the party. It matters little now, and there should be no worry or accusation over it. It is past.

Two men left us that very day, starting back up the coast. We watched them go.

"Are there any more cowards?" asked Blue Jay.

No one spoke. We all knew that those were brave men who simply disagreed with their leader. But no one wanted to anger Blue Jay at that point. Maybe we . . . no, never mind.

That was the last that we saw of those two. I have been told that they have not returned here, so they must be mourned as dead. *Aiee!*

Now, Blue Jay was almost elated. He remarked that now he expected nothing but loyalty. Certainly, that seemed likely. No one would challenge him now. But the party was alarmingly small. Only eight, even counting the woman. There would be only seven on the way home. Six, after we left Caddo Talker with his own people. But that was all in the future. For now, a decision had been reached, even without discussion. It had happened so quickly that I almost wondered how. Now, we were committed to go on.

Blue Jay began to ask Flower of the country ahead. She kept assuring us that it would be good traveling, though I had doubts. She explained that the distant mountains come much nearer the sea there. Any strip of swampy country would be quite narrow, and the land would begin to rise, drier and cooler than on the coast.

"You will see," she insisted.

Well, it was not quite like that, but in a way, she did

speak truth. I still think she did not really try to mislead us. At least, not about that.

We hurried to get ready to travel now. It would only be a few days, maybe less, until the next storm.

"Where do we leave the sea?" I asked.

We had talked before of the fact that the heaviest rain falls on the coast there. If we could leave the sea and start to climb into the hills, we would not be so bothered by the frequent rains. But again, she was vague. I do not know why, but I think she was just uncertain. It had been several years since she had seen this area.

"I will know when I see it," she answered in hand-signs.

Apparently she was looking for some landmark or other, and I was never sure. We started on, keeping a careful watch on the sky. Our mood was not the best, because we were still shaken by the quarrel that had taken two of our number.

Except, of course, for Blue Jay. He was almost jubilant, striding ahead with confidence, happy to be involved with a quest so important.

We stopped that night in time to withdraw a little way from the crashing breakers of the sea. Flower taught us to make a sort of shelter from the big leaves of some of the palm trees, and we settled in for the night. It was damp and uncomfortable and it seemed better to sleep outside. The disadvantage to that was that the mosquitos were large and fierce. Flower suggested that we sleep downwind from the fire, which helped a little, but not much.

I tried to wrap myself in my sleeping-robe to avoid the bite of the creatures. But it was hot and damp, and every tiny bit of exposed skin was searched out by the hordes of mosquitos. My face, ears, my hand which held the robe in place were all targets. One even bit me in the part of my hair, in that slender stripe of skin.

I woke next morning with swollen eyes and ears, and I could close my fist only with difficulty. I longed for my lodge on the open plain, with the bottom of the lodge skin rolled up like a lifted skirt to let the breeze flow through.

I almost wished that I had turned back with the two rebels, but I said nothing. I privately tried a spell or two to try to get a sign for the future, but could not tell much. I did not want to cast the bones again, because it would become public, and I was not certain that I wanted to see what they would show.

My worst sign, though, was very disconcerting. When I rose, I put my hand to my chest to adjust the Spanish bit, my elk-dog amulet. The hand came away with red stains on the fingers, where I had touched the bit. Startled, I looked again at the bit.

It had always been of highly polished metal, with tiny glittering dangles of silver. They always reminded me of the flash of minnows in a clear prairie stream. But the main body of the bit itself and the ring that held the elk-dog medicine were kept bright, also, by wearing and by handling.

Today, it was not so. The entire bit, except for the silver dangles, was *red*. Almost blood-red, in fact, with a powdery rust that had stained my hands and my buckskins.

This is not a good sign, I thought.

I spent some time in polishing it, rubbing it with sand and then greasing it whenever we killed something for food that had any fat. Even so, it continued to turn red. It *was* a bad sign. Worse than I realized at the time.

16

The rains returned before we left that camp, and we spent two miserable, sodden days there. Our hearts were very heavy, and I am sure that some of the others wondered, as I did, about the two who had left us. Maybe, even, why we had not gone back *with* them.

Much of this time we were hungry, too. We could not hunt in the rain, for our bowstrings were soft and limp, even if we could have tolerated the downpour and the wind. We killed one large water bird on the beach the second day. It was about the size of a goose or turkey. It was tough and strong-tasting, rather fishy, but it was meat. We had much trouble building fires all during this rain-soaked period, but usually, just as we began to despair, Antelope would succeed. He was better with the fire-sticks than any of us.

The constant moisture also caused red, itchy spots on our skins. These were dry and scaly, and were only one of the great discomforts in that place.

What? How can the wet make dry patches on the skin? *Aiee*, I do not know, but it does. Some are round with a reddened rim, others more mottled. When these are scratched, white scaly powder falls off. These places healed, though, when we found sunlight again. But that was long after.

Mosquitos were a constant problem in that rainy season. I mentioned them before, did I not? Yes. Flower had warned us of this, but we were not prepared. With the rain, you see, every little low spot, every curled leaf, every hollow in a rock held water. It does not soak in or go away, as it does here, it just lies there. Soon, every little puddle was teeming with the wiggle-tails that turn into mosquitos. We never saw such a thing.

White Flower constantly reassured us that it would be better in the highlands away from the sea, and we believed her. The problem was how to get there when the rain only paused for a little while and then started again.

White Flower woke us early on the morning that clearing began. It was before sunrise, but we could see that there were stars overhead, and only a few scattered clouds. We quickly rolled out of our sleeping-robes, which were damp and uncomfortable anyway. Flower led the way, and by full light, we were following a faint game trail nearly due west, away from the sea.

My feelings were mixed. The prospect of leaving the sea was good, because I had grown weary of the constant sand in my moccasins and the stickiness of salt on my skin and my garments. The thought of leaving those discomforts was good. Flower also promised that we would soon be leaving the stinking, swampy lowlands, with their strange spirits, mosquitos, dangerous creatures, and sicknesses. We had not even encountered *that* danger. Not yet . . .

On the other hand, I regretted somewhat leaving the shore. That is strange, I know, to regret leaving a place that you have come to hate. The idea of freshwater streams to drink, and to bathe and cleanse our skins of the salt and sand was good. The regret was because we were leaving our only familiar landmark. It had not always been a good landmark, it is true. That coast is so irregular, so dotted with islands offshore. . . . Once we traveled for most of a day, thinking we were on the shore, and then came to the end of it. We were following a long finger of land that merely came to an end in the water. Fortunately, the strip of water between that and the real shore was narrow and shallow, and we were able to wade across. Otherwise we would have lost at least a day. But enough . . .

The loss of the sea bothered me, I suppose, because it was the only far horizon we had seen for a long time. You know, maybe, the trapped feeling when you have been traveling or camping in a forest? It is a closed-in feeling, with trees and hills and bushes. You cannot see any distance at all. All of these things that prevent a clear and healthy view of the world seem to be pushing in around you. The spirit of such a place is foreign to us. The People begin to long for the freedom of the wind across open grassland. We want to be able to *see* the span of a day's travel ahead of us. We need to stretch our eyes.

The lack of ability to do that bothers us, fetters our spirit, and takes some of our freedom. Living then becomes like dwelling in the mud lodges of the Growers, with only one opening, and none of the spirit of the open prairie carried on the breeze through our lodges. We can raise our lodge covers in summer. . . . Forgive me, friends. Forgive my tears, also. Only, it is so good to be back in my home country.

Anyway, the sea had been my only look at the distant rim of Earth. Even though it was water and not grass, I suppose I had used it to retain my sanity in this world gone mad. I hated to leave it. To one who is starving, any food looks good. Maybe our spirits were starving. At least, I now think they were fighting for our lives.

As we traveled that morning, there was one other event that stands out in my memory. Flower was in the lead, as I said. I was maybe third or fourth in line. Suddenly there was a loud hiss or snarl. It is a sound hard to describe, like the hiss of a snake or one of our big snapping turtles in an attitude of threatening. Even the snake's hiss can be a frightening thing, but think how much more so when the creature involved is three or four paces long!

There beside the trail was one of those giant thunder-lizards. I had not seen one before that was completely out of the water. *Aiee*, it was frightening. The great pink-white mouth with its rows of teeth was open wide. It looked big enough to swallow a man. The lizard stood on short thick legs, braced and ready to charge.

We were reaching for our weapons, but Flower gave the hand-sign to wait. She was nearest, and since she was more familiar with such things, we waited.

"Move slowly," she signed. "Follow me."

Very carefully, she moved at a steady pace, past the threatening creature. One by one, we followed. We were passing within three, maybe four paces of this danger, but

156

it remained motionless. Once, one of the men slipped in the muddy path and made a sudden move. The lizard gave a dreadful hiss and turned in that direction, but did not attack.

I had been in a cold sweat when I passed it. You realize that these animals can run as fast as a man, at least for a little way. It could have killed at least one of us, if it had chosen.

We all passed safely, though, and gathered at a little clearing beyond. There was great relief.

Now Flower explained, with signs and through Caddo Talker.

"This was a female defending her nest," she told us.

"But we saw no young," a man observed.

"True. They are eggs."

This was a thing of great wonder, that so big a creature would lay eggs. Yet, we know that some of our lizards do, and some snakes.

These creatures, Flower went on, place their eggs in a pile of rotting plant material to warm them until the young hatch.

"See?" she pointed.

We had not noticed before, but now that it had been pointed out to us, I wondered how we missed it. We had been occupied with watching the lizard, I suppose. Behind the hissing creature, up against a couple of trees was a sort of trashy pile of vegetation, steaming in the damp air. It was nearly as high as my knees and a pace or two across.

"But I see no eggs!" someone protested.

"True," answered Flower when the question had been relayed through Caddo Talker. "She covers them, and pulls off a little or piles it back on to keep them warmer or cooler."

We marveled at this.

"Do your people hunt these creatures?" someone asked.

"Sometimes. Not much. I did not want to shoot this one, because even in dying they are very dangerous, and we had no place to run."

Caddo Talker translated, and everyone laughed.

I wondered about the young and how the mother cares for them. She does not, Flower said. Once they are hatched and moving well, she leaves them and they scatter. I thought that many probably do not survive, but are eaten by some of the hunters of this forest. Flower said that this is true.

"How big are they?" I asked.

"When they hatch? About this big," she answered, holding her hands a little way apart. About a hand's widest span, maybe.

Later that day, we killed one of these lizards for meat. It was not big . . . only about a pace long. Yes, I know that is big. But for these thunder-lizards, that is a small one. Flower prepared it for us, and it was good. She said that the best part was the tail, and this is true, maybe. Just as we love the hump-ribs of the buffalo. *Aiee*, I missed that delicacy!

We traveled on, and by evening when we stopped to camp we could see that the land was rising. Flower spoke truth, and we *were* leaving the sodden lowlands behind. We ate the little thunder-lizard, as I mentioned before, and settled in for the night.

I was a little more optimistic now. For one thing, Antelope's fire had started quite easily. That may have been just a fortunate circumstance, or he may have had better tinder. I know that he had been trying to learn from Flower about what plants might make good fire-starters here. So, I do not know. But it seemed like a good sign, anyway. The night was clear, the stars bright. That was good, too, because it helped me establish direction. I found that I had been wrong, and would have placed north somewhere in the northeast. I have always had a poor sense of direction in wooded or hilly places. There are no landmarks. But, no matter. I spoke of that already, I guess.

By morning I began to wonder if our good signs were not yet another sign of the treachery of this strange land. I was awakened by the cry of one of the big spotted jaguars. I built up the fire a little bit. It is a comfort to have the light, and whether it keeps the hunting cat at bay or not, it helps to think so.

Others were awake, too, and we sat listening to the sounds of the night. It occurred to me that practically none of them were sounds that we would hear at home. They had become familiar to us now, but suddenly the whole world seemed strange to me. We had left the familiar spirits of the prairie and plains far behind, and were surrounded by spirits that were strange and unfamiliar to us. I felt lost and afraid. Why had we come here?

Yes, I had been as eager as any at first, but now I felt that we were dealing with things beyond us. I wished that our leader had been not quite so intent on this exploration. I mean to speak no ill of Blue Jay, friends. As I have said, he is a great leader, and my friend. We all supported him in his quest, except for the disagreements I have mentioned, and those were proper. But I am afraid that now I was beginning to have doubts. There seemed no end to this. Travel, stop, shoot some strange creature for food, become drenched by the seasonal rain, bitten by mosquitos, struggle to start a fire, sleep poorly in the steamy heat, get up with the day and struggle on. I devoutly wished that morning that we had turned back with the two others. Maybe I would talk of it with Blue Jay.

My thoughts were interrupted by a man who came to me, a look of wonder on his face in the firelight.

"Dog's Leg," he said, pointing. "He says he is freezing."

Now, my friends, it was a hot night. Damp, steaming . . . Our problem had been whether to wrap tightly in our sleeping-robes to avoid the hungry mosquitos. That was sweaty and uncomfortable, but so were the hundreds of bites. Most of us alternated, uncomfortably hot for a while, then a little cooler, but bitten mercilessly.

But Dog's Leg . . . I went over to where he lay, tightly wrapped in his thick buffalo robe. He was shivering with a chill, unable to hold still against the powerful tremors. He looked up, his eyes glassy in the firelight.

"He asked to borrow my robe to keep warm," said another man.

Something was dreadfully wrong. The rest of us were sweating and slapping at mosquitos, but here was poor Dog's Leg, wrapped in his thick furry robe, shivering with cold and trying to borrow another robe to warm himself.

This was not a good sign.

17

We could not go on with one of us so ill. We camped there, where we were. Before the day was done, Dog's Leg's chill was over, but it was replaced by something worse. He lay limp and lifeless, his skin hot to touch. It was terrible to see, and even more distressing that he seemed not even to know us.

I tried some of the medicines from my pack, and sang some chants, but I had little confidence that it would help. Confidence is important, both on the part of the healer and the patient. I had no confidence. . . . I freely admit it. I was trying to treat something completely unknown to me.

As for the sick man, I think that at that point, he did not even know his name. All my procedures failed, and I was afraid he was dying.

I must admit, I did not know what to do. Sometimes a holy man's medicine works, sometimes not. But in dealing with the illnesses here, usually we know what to expect. There is at least some feeling as to whether the chants and remedies will succeed. You all know that some injuries will seldom be helped by all our medicine. And some things that appear hopeless will respond well to the appropriate medicine.

This was a strange illness, that which had struck down our friend. It is not unheard of, a fever with chills. We see it often. But rarely does it swing to these extremes. Shaking, teeth-chattering chills alternating with the burning fever. During the hot times, Dog's Leg was delirious, unknowing who or where he was. We wiped his face with cloths White Flower had dampened in water.

Flower said something to Caddo Talker, he answered her, and their discussion became more intense as they talked. Then he turned to me.

"The woman knows what this is. It is a thing of the swampy country. A spirit of some sort, I think she is saying."

I had been afraid of this. Since the first of these stinking damp places, I had feared that against unfamiliar spirits, my powers would not work. And, my friends, I am made to think that the spirits in such a place are bad, evil. I can understand dangers that we encounter in our grassland, our Sacred Hills, where the air is clean, and the breeze refreshing when we sit in front of our lodges in the cool of the evening. . . . Forgive me . . . I am rambling like an old man.

"I thought so," I told Caddo Talker. "My medicine does not have powers against it."

"But she knows what to do," he told me. "There is a tree, if she can find one."

"A tree?"

"Yes. She needs a part of it."

"Fruit? Seeds? Leaves?" I asked, eager for whatever was needed.

"No, she says the outside, the skin. Something like that."

"Ah! The bark. It is good! Can she find such a tree?"

"She says yes. Shall some of us go with her?"

He asked this of Blue Jay.

"Of course," Jay said. "You go, and take two others, to protect you and the woman."

I had a moment of alarm at splitting the party in half again, but it was necessary. We had to do something, because it was plain that Dog's Leg was dying.

The four quickly gathered weapons and left the camp. It seemed very lonely, with only three of us who were in possession of our senses. We wondered where Dog's Leg's spirit was, when it did not seem to be in him. His eyes were blank, empty, like when you look into the doorway of an empty lodge and there is nobody home.

He appeared worse to me, the fever worse now than it had been the last time it rose. This was not sudden, you understand. Maybe a day . . . I do not remember. But between the fevers came a time of weakness, when he was limp, so tired he could not move or eat. Then the chill, with shaking. *Aiee*, it would seem that the shaking would throw off the robes that we had piled on him for warmth. This, of course, while we were sweating with the heat. Our hearts were heavy for our brother.

White Flower and the others returned after what

165

seemed a long time. It was good to see them. There are times when a person needs numbers for protection. In case of an attack, or an unplanned fire on the prairie. There are other times when it is not so much for defense or protection as for comfort. It is a comfort of the spirit. When one's heart is heavy, another spirit nearby helps us. Like a mother's arms comfort her babe. It was like that. All of our spirits lifted, those who had gone after the medicine-tree as well as those who stayed behind. Now we were eight again, and our spirits rose in gladness.

Flower and one of the men carried armfuls of bark that had been stripped from trees. The others had remained free to use their weapons if necessary. I was amazed at the quantity of bark that they carried, and asked about it through Caddo Talker. There was some conversation between him and Flower, and then he turned back to me.

"She says that it does not take much," he explained, "but we must all take it. Not just Dog's Leg."

"But we are not sick!"

"That is true. But when these spirits find a village or a camp, like ours, they sometimes strike everyone."

This was bad news. We have some sicknesses like that, of course, which jump from one to another. I had not even thought that this might be that way. It was enough evil that one of our party was struck down without the threat of that spirit or others leaping from one of us to another.

"Ask her," I requested, "whether this bad spirit jumps directly from the sick to the healthy."

That led to greater discussion. It is possible, of course, to talk of simple ideas with gestures and hand-signs and a few words. This was a more complicated thing, and there was still a problem of translation.

Finally Caddo Talker turned to me again.

"I am not sure what she is telling, Uncle. She says it is not dangerous to be near Dog's Leg. But, when the hot-cold spirit finds such a home, it tells others. We are all in danger."

"The woman, too?"

"Yes. She says she has drunk this medicine many times."

"Ah! It is used as a potion?"

"Yes. A sort of tea."

I had been looking at the strips of bark, smelling them. There was little odor. I touched the tip of my tongue to the damp surface of one of the strips. It was bitter . . . *aiee*, like a mixture of gall and ashes, maybe. I quickly understood why it must be used as a drink. No one could stand to chew such evil-tasting stuff, but it could be swallowed quickly in a tea. It was plain how it worked. Such medicine was foul enough to drive out any bad spirit. I made a wry face, and White Flower laughed, but not much. The situation was too desperate.

She began to chop and separate the tender layers of bark from the rougher outside, and I sat down to help her. I was familiar with such preparation, of course, because of my own profession. She smiled and nodded when she saw my work.

"It is good," she signed.

She had apparently told Caddo Talker of the need for hot water, and he had begun to heat some to have it ready. Ah, I had not mentioned, I guess . . . Flower had a little pot made of metal! She used it sometimes to cook in. The Spanish use such things, and her people have had much contact with Spanish. She could put this little pot with water in it right on the fire!

When the water began to bubble, Flower tossed in pieces of her prepared bark and set it aside to cool.

"Tell me of this tree," I asked Caddo Talker.

"It is just a tree," he told me. "A small tree. I think it is always green, maybe. But most trees are, in this place."

"Would Flower tell me of it? Its name, show it to me?"

Caddo Talker shrugged. "I will ask her."

The woman nodded, and seemed pleased. I wondered if she had some sort of special powers . . . a holy woman of some sort. She had impressed us all with her wit, her strength, and her wisdom. It remained to be seen if this medicine worked.

While it was cooling, we talked through Caddo Talker.

"How is this tree called?" I asked.

She answered quickly, without translation, for I had signed. The hand-signs for such a question are simple, and she understood well.

"It is called *sin-ko-na*," she answered, in a mix of hand-signs and mouth-talk.

Then she went on to tell, through Caddo Talker, how it was brought from the south, used in trade, and only in the past few lifetimes was grown here, for the purpose of driving out these swamp spirits.

"This is like a crop, for Growers?" I asked.

"I think not, Uncle," Caddo Talker said. "I think it is *allowed* to grow."

Many of the plants used by the People are so, as you know. We use plums and different berries, but do not plant as Growers do. Who planted the first ones, the first plums, for instance? No one, maybe. They were planted at Creation. But sometimes, people help to plant things in new places, too. And, I have noticed that many things that we now use have come from the south, as this *sin-ko-na* tree has. But I am rambling again. It is only that I was so impressed by the powerful medicine of this tree in holding off the evil of the swamp spirits.

I asked if she could teach me to find and identify this tree, and she was quite agreeable.

But first things first. The *sin-ko-na* tea was cooling now, and she took a gourd spoon to put a little into the mouth of Dog's Leg. His fever was hot, and I hoped that this would help it. Flower gently cradled his head in her arm, and put the dipper to his lips as one would feed a child. He took a sip and made a wry face. I could understand that, because I had tasted the bitter bark. Remember, though, Dog's Leg was delirious with the fever. The evil spirit in him made him struggle wildly, and he knocked the gourd aside, spilling the precious fluid. At the same time, his struggles seemed to be too much for his weakened body. He was seized with a spasm that shook him all over, and then went suddenly limp. He died in the woman's arms.

I saw her tears come, and was impressed once more by this courageous woman. She had tried to help, and failed.

"It is too late," she signed, bowing her head.

There was a reaction on the part of the others that caught me completely by surprise. A low mutter, as we might expect, but the first one to speak uttered words that I could not believe.

"She killed him!"

"No," I said. "She tried to help!"

"But he was alive before she gave him that drink!"

Aiee, what to do? If there was anything that we did not need, it was a dispute among ourselves.

The argument rose in temper and in volume.

"She wanted us all to drink that!" yelled one man. "She wants to kill us all. Probably to feed us to her tribe!"

My friends, this was a time of great sorrow!

169

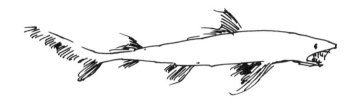

18

It was the last thing we needed, of course, to be fighting among ourselves. The unexpected death of poor Dog's Leg had caused great sorrow, and sometimes a heavy heart seeks a reason.

I was very concerned for the safety of Flower. She sat, puzzled at the angry faces before her, still holding our brother's head in her lap. Her eyes were filled with sadness as she looked helplessly from one to another. It was my thought that she did not realize the danger that threatened her.

"She is trying to kill us all," one said again. "We should kill *her* first!"

"True," said another. "Look! There are only six of us left."

I noticed, even at the time, that Caddo Talker was not counted in that last speech. But he was not one to be ignored. I was beginning to see the mark of a leader in this young man. Calmly, without any excitement, he stepped over to a position that placed him between White Flower and the man who had spoken so angrily. Caddo Talker made no threatening moves at all, but I noticed that the ax at his waist was ready in case he needed it.

"Your talk is foolish," he said gently. "She tried to save him, but it was too late. A cure must start early to be effective. Is it not so, Walks in the Sun?"

I nodded, still wondering what would happen next.

"Now, we must all drink this tea to prevent such an illness." He turned to the woman. "True?" he asked, and repeated his statement in Caddo. At least, it appeared so.

Flower nodded, and Caddo Talker reached down to pick up the dropped dipper-spoon. He filled it from the little pot and drank the tea quickly, then looked around the circle to see the reaction. It was quiet. Even those who had talked the loudest had to be impressed by this show of confidence. I saw his eyes meet those of White Flower, and there was a flash of understanding there that I had not noticed. Maybe he had said something else to her, something we had missed. A warning, maybe. She sat very still, but nodded in approval at his action.

Now I knew that he was right, and needed support. I took the dipper and drank a dose of the vile-tasting stuff . . . *aiee*, it is bitter! Flower nodded, pleased. I then handed the gourd to Blue Jay. He looked surprised, but drank without hesitation. He, in turn, filled the dipper again and handed it to Flower herself. It was a good move, one befitting a leader. If she would drink, it would certainly wipe out the suspicion that hovered in the heads of the dissenters.

She drank and handed the dipper back to Blue Jay. Jay held it out toward the others. There were three, you remember, who had not yet drunk. For a little while, no one moved. Then one stepped forward, Lean Antelope, always a thoughtful one.

"I have doubts," he said, "but my fear of this evil swamp spirit is greater. Give it to me."

He took a sip at first, made a wry face, and then manfully took the rest in one gulp. He shook his head and handed the gourd to the others. At least, he tried to do so. They stood unmoved in their refusal and did not drink. Not at that time.

Now I must explain a little more. I do not want it to appear that I am criticizing our brothers for their decision. What I am saying is this: It was *their* decision to make, their choice. Each of us has this right. I told them that I was made to feel we should drink this, but I cannot force others to think as I do, and I should not try. So, two of us chose not to drink.

White Flower, too, tried to tell them, but it was no use. She shook her head sadly, feeling bad because of the risk they chose to take.

"We must all drink this tea each day," she said in hand-signs.

We nodded agreement, but the two who did not wish to drink seemed even more certain now, at the threat of daily doses.

"How long must we do this? How many days?" I asked.

Flower was vague, as she sometimes was about many things. I am made to think that the thinking of her people is a little different. With no winter season for which they must prepare, there is not the same urgency to prepare and store food against the Moon of Hunger. Weather changes do not seem so important to them, maybe. So tomorrow does not have the same importance as it does to us. So, in answer to how long, she only replied, "As long as we need it."

Well, I decided, we can face that when the time comes. We now know more of this swamp spirit, and we can learn more yet. I would wait and see. And maybe their way and ours are not so different, after all.

Of more immediate concern was the preparation of our brother Dog's Leg for burial. It was of great concern to us that his bones should rest not in the sod of the Sacred Hills but in this strange land with its threatening spirits. We talked of this that night around our fire, after we had cared for him and sung the Song of Mourning.

"Will his spirit be trapped here?" Jay asked me.

"I think not," I told him. "What do you say, Caddo Talker?"

I thought it good to see what his people might think. You know, the Head Splitters' beliefs are a little different from ours. They do not fight at night, because the spirit of one who dies in the dark may lose its way in the darkness and wander forever. But I do not recall ever hearing of what happens to a spirit who tries to cross over in a different *place*.

Caddo Talker thought a little while and finally answered, slowly.

"I am made to think," he said thoughtfully, "that it does not matter. My people, and yours too, travel a great deal. We have no fears of where we die, if it is our time. It is as easy to cross over in one place as another. After the crossing-over journey, maybe it is all one place, no? It is the journey that is important."

I had never thought of it in just that way, but this seemed good. As we considered, it seemed to be more important that Dog's Leg have all of our help that he could. We had wrapped and tied his body in his sleeping-robe and built a scaffold for him. We had sung for him. A small supply of food and water and tobacco, along with his weapons, were placed beside him. It does not take long to make the crossing, I think, because we leave only a little food, no? That is what we have been taught.

We decided to stay an extra day, however, to sing for our brother and maybe give him an easier crossing.

Now, I am sure you wonder at why we were more concerned for this brother than the others we had lost. The one who was eaten, those who disappeared . . . I want the relatives of all these men to know that we did for them what we could. We sang for them. We were not able to give their bones proper burial, as we did for Dog's Leg. We did not *have* their bones. I am made to think, though, that we made their crossing easier with the guidance of our songs. I do not apologize for myself or the others. We did what we could.

So we stayed the extra day. White Flower was not completely pleased with this, as she was nearing home. But she put the day to good use. With the aid of a couple of the men, she gathered and prepared a quantity of the tree bark that had come too late for Dog's Leg. I went with her, and she showed me how to identify the tree. I was surprised at its size, not much bigger than our prairie dogwood. It was good to have this knowledge, though I hope I never have use for it again. I have no desire ever to set foot in that terrible country again.

Yet it does have a majestic beauty about it. Not the jungles. I did not care for that. But the land into which we were coming as we traveled away from the sea. There were hills rising ahead of us. From time to time we could see much farther, far enough that we could see the blue of more distant hills. Mountains, even.

"That is my home!" Flower signed proudly.

I could see why she had been anxious to return.

There is always promise in a view of distant hills and unknown places. I am made to think that maybe this is why the People move from one place to another all our lives. What great adventures, more exciting than today's, lie just over that next rise? I am made to think that all people feel this, except maybe Growers, who must stay where their crops are planted. But maybe even they . . . never mind. What I am trying to say is that now, as the hills rose before us, I was feeling this feeling for the first time in a long while. The air was better, and it tasted good to breathe it in. It was still the rainy season, but it seemed to me that there was less of the water-soaked sodden feeling in the air, less of a squishing feel underfoot when we walked.

I wondered a little what season it might be at home. Summer, surely. The Sun Dance might even be over. *Aiee,* how could we have so deceived ourselves for so long? How could we have let this happen to us? A year before, if anyone had told me that I would be a party to such a crazy thing . . . But, here we were. I tried to console myself with three things.

First, we had learned much. It was the adventure of a lifetime. Next, we had helped this unfortunate young woman, who without us would still be a slave-wife in a strange land. Or worse. I wanted to think that if one of our women fell on evil times and was taken far from home,

178

there would be someone who would help her, as we had helped this woman. I admit, that was not our original purpose, but it had come to be so, as we came to love and respect our companion.

But lastly, I felt better about our entire situation for yet another reason, one that was growing stronger by the day. Soon we would have accomplished our last purpose, the return of White Flower to her own people. At least, her own country. Then, we would start home.

I cherished that thought. I was thinking ahead, using what we now knew of the seasons here. We would be on the return journey during the winter, the dry season, and traveling would be good. We would be reaching familiar territory as spring came to the prairie. Maybe we would be following the awakening northward, as we had followed autumn south so long ago.

My thoughts were good as I sat by the fire and watched the stars. It was a clear night, one of few we had seen recently. A voice interrupted the private journey in my head and brought me back to reality.

"Walks in the Sun!" said Caddo Talker. "The woman says you should come. One is sick."

"Who?"

"Snake-Road."

He was, of course, one of the men who had refused the medicine-tea. He looked up at me with fear and helplessness in his eyes. His teeth chattered with the chill as he clasped his robe around him. I turned to White Flower.

"The medicine?" I asked in signs.

"We will give it, but I fear it will be too late," she signed.

From what I had learned of this hot-cold swamp spirit so far, I was afraid so, too.

19

Snake-Road had fallen ill next. At least, I think it was that way. I speak his name because there is another by that name that I know. This was a strange man. We knew little about him, even after the closeness of our quest together. He was a loner who had no family. I think he was at his best when he was alone, following a dim trail through the prairie or the woods. He had been invaluable to us. But I am getting ahead of my story again.

We were well away from the sea, a few days' travel, and the weather was so much better that our spirits soared like the eagle. Flower assured us that we were nearing her people now, and her excitement, too, was a joy to us. She insisted that we continue to drink her bark tea each day, though we were becoming careless about it. At least we were until Snake-Road fell ill with the hot-cold illness. I was surprised, for I thought we had left it behind. I did not understand.

"This sickness has followed us?" I asked White Flower in signs.

She shrugged and spread her hands in a helpless gesture.

"He did not drink the tea."

It may seem strange for me to tell you that I had overlooked that. It was a danger that I thought was behind us, so I had put it out of my mind and had not even noticed the connection. The one who fell ill was the one who had not taken the potion. My thoughts turned to the other one, the man who had talked of killing the woman. He had been very quiet for several days. Now would be a time to watch how he would react. Would he try to do harm to Flower?

I mentioned this to Blue Jay, and he agreed.

"We must watch her closely, in case he does something stupid. Let us warn Antelope and Caddo Talker."

"I think Caddo Talker needs no warning," I observed. "He is always with her anyway."

Blue Jay chuckled and nodded. Those two had been growing closer ever since the battle with the snake, I guess. Antelope said nothing when we spoke to him, but only nodded.

As it happened, the reaction that we feared did not occur. The warrior who had refused to drink earlier seemed completely convinced now. He approached White Flower very humbly and asked that he be permitted to take the medicine with the others. She willingly provided it. The rest of us also became much more faithful with our own dosage, as you might well imagine.

I was eager to learn more of this illness now. That night I sat with Flower and Caddo Talker and questioned her at great length. We used both hand-signs and the clumsy translation, which was becoming easier, however. Flower was very quick at language. She had had to learn several tongues during her captivity, I suppose.

"Tell me of this hot-cold illness," I asked. "I do not understand . . . it follows us?"

"For a while, sometimes," she told me. "I do not know why, but some fall sick later, after contact with the swamp spirits."

"How long do they follow us?" I asked.

"I do not know. Maybe as long as a moon or more. It is hard to tell whether the illness is from a moon ago, or maybe a new spirit has found us. And there are different kinds."

"Different kinds?" I was puzzled.

"Yes. One spirit brings the hot-cold only every three days. This kind, I think, is more dangerous. There is much of this that I do not know, Walks in the Sun."

"But the tree bark helps all the different kinds?"

"Yes, of that I am sure. It is good to drive away the bad spirits. But sometimes, the spirit it too powerful."

It was too powerful for poor Snake-Road. Within another day he was dead.

Before we had hardly begun to build his scaffold, the other man who had refused the medicine fell ill, also. He vomited continually and was seized with spasms in his belly and with dysentery. Flower went to fetch her little pot of medicine-tea and returned with a shocked expression on her face.

"He drank it all!" she reported. "I do not know whether he is sick with the bad spirit or with the medicine."

We never did know. He seemed somewhat better in the morning, but then we had a new problem. Should we give him more medicine? He developed the chills and fever, and the cramps continued.

"Maybe he has more than one bad swamp spirit," suggested Flower.

That was never answered for us, either. His face quickly became drawn, his eyes sunken and blank. Before we finished the ceremonial songs of mourning for Snake-Road, we had another scaffold to build and more songs to sing. It was a time of great sadness.

Of course that delayed us further, which we did not regret. The delay, I mean. We regretted the losses of our brothers, even though we had disagreed. Flower was very understanding, and mourned with us, though I knew that she was impatient, being this close to home.

On top of all of this, it rained again, for most of a day. This prevented travel, and we huddled again under our robes and our makeshift shelters, waiting.

But we soon found that Flower spoke truth when she said that hers was a better climate. This upland country drains well, so there are not the sodden flatlands where water gathers and swamp creatures breed and spirits of sickness lurk. Half a day after the rain stopped, we could travel again.

Another day and we came to a heavier forest. There were different trees and plants that grew here, different than in the jungle behind us. The air was better, though I still did not feel comfortable in a place with no far horizons.

"I know where we are, now," Flower signed with a smile. "Tomorrow I will show you something."

She would not speak further of it. I wondered what it might be that would make her so vague. Her people? No, surely if that had been her secret, she would have simply said so. It occurred to me that of all the strange and impossible things that she had told us, most of them had been quite true. I tried to think. What fanciful creatures, what feature of her land might lie ahead? After her help in fighting the swamp spirits' threat, I was ready to believe anything she said. Well, almost. True, she had saved our lives. It was sad that those who had doubted her had now paid with theirs. But there were still things that she had told us that were, by all reason, impossible. Of course, I had thought that about the mouthless anteater, too. Well, we would see.

The next afternoon, when the day was growing short, Blue Jay suggested that we stop for the night.

"A little farther," Flower signed.

She had not shown us anything very remarkable. Bright parrots, flowers in the trees. They were beautiful, but I had the feeling that these were not the things that she wished to show us. There must be something more.

"A good camp, ahead," she indicated.

"It is good," Jay signed back. "You lead."

Flower took the lead, striding with long legs along the trail as confidently as any man. Once more I thought that such a woman would be appreciated in our plains tribes. She could let her wisdom and strength grow and flourish there. I found myself hoping that her people would appreciate such a woman. I did not know.

It must have been almost sunset when we entered a large open space. Flower indicated that this was the site that she sought, and we began to prepare camp quickly. There was little light left.

187

I began to gather some fuel for our fire, and as I did so, I took a look around. There was forest on all sides of us, but the clearing was maybe a hundred paces across, with smaller trees and shrubs here and there. It appeared quite flat, but at the far side of the open space there was a strangely shaped little hill. It rose straight out of the flat place, steep on all sides. It is hard to describe this hill . . . well, like a lodge. Yes, its shape was like a giant skin lodge such as we use, but big, big! More than two bowshots across its base, and about as tall. It was covered with trees and vines, and I saw, or rather heard, small creatures like squirrels scampering and chattering in the growth on that steep hillside. I raised my eyes toward its top, which was flattened. It was like our lodges, as I said, but as if someone cut the top off to flatten the top. Cut off the poles and the skin cover below the smoke flaps. *Aiee*, I am making no sense. The lodge would fall down. But I am talking only of the shape of this hill, no? It was flat on top.

Then I saw something that filled me with excitement and a little fear. There was a great lodge there on the top of that hill, bigger than any ever seen by the People. It was built of great blocks of stone, and though it was partly hidden by trees and vines, I could tell that it was huge. Bigger than the Governor's Palace on the Plaza in Santa Fe. Bigger than the whole fort that the French built in our lifetimes at the town of the Cenzas. Some of you were there . . . yes, bigger than that.

I was standing there, staring openmouthed, when I heard a chuckle at my elbow. It was White Flower.

"You see, Walks in the Sun?"

"What is it?" I gasped.

"This is the Sacred Place of the Old Ones," she signed. "I told you."

I was so astonished that I had forgotten. Yes, she had told of this. I had assumed that she lied. I now stood and gazed at the nearly hidden stone posts, each much taller than a man, maybe three times as tall. The white stone gleamed in the fading light.

"Look at the hill," the woman signed, pointing to the hill itself.

I stepped forward, not knowing what she meant. A hill is a hill, no? What I found was even more astonishing, maybe, than the great longhouse at the top. This hill was composed of steps, great blocks of stone, with dirt under them. There were places where a stone had crumbled or fallen away, and I could see the dirt and smaller stones inside. I now saw, too, that the hill was square at the base, not round as I had thought. Its lines had been obscured by the brushy growth and the failing light. It still had not completely come to me, the meaning of it all, but now it suddenly struck me. Not only had the great lodge at the top of the hill been built by hands, but *the hill itself*! The very idea was so strange, so foreign to all that we know. And what great powers these Old Ones must have had! My own gifts as a holy man seemed insignificant and useless here.

"How? Why?" I signed in wonder.

Since both signs are the same, this came through to White Flower simply as a question, though a very big question. What, where, when, how, *why*? All at once. Maybe it is significant that I could ask it all with a single hand-sign.

"No one knows," she answered seriously, "except the Old Ones. It was a holy place for them."

And still is, I thought. I could feel the presence of their powerful spirits reaching out to me.

"I must climb the hill," I signed.

"No, not tonight," Flower signed. "It will soon be dark, and there are dangers. Snakes, maybe."

I agreed to wait, but it was not easy. I was strongly drawn to this place of the spirit. I could feel its importance.

Reluctantly, I turned back to where Lean Antelope had just kindled his fire. Cheery little flames were curling up through damp wood, and a column of smoke, thin as a lodge pole and as straight, rose straight toward the sky. There seemed something significant in that.

I reached into my pack to draw out a pinch of tobacco. With a devout prayer I offered it on the growing fire. This was a place of powerful spirits, and we dared not offend them. We also needed their help, I thought. Soon we would start home and would need every bit of help that any kindly spirits could give us.

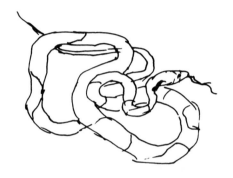

20

I slept little that night. I was filled with the excitement of discovery, and what I might be able to learn here. The presence of the Old Ones' spirits, or *some* spirits, was very strong, and I longed for more.

Finally the exhaustion of a hard day overcame me, and I slept. Then came the dreams, like none I had ever experienced. It seemed to me in my mind that I was taken back to the time of the Old Ones. Not *our* Old Ones, who built dwellings and left paintings and carvings on the rocks and in the caves. *These* Old Ones, those of White Flower's country. The nation that built the great lodge and the hill that it stood upon.

It was the sort of dream that one knows is a dream, and sees the events as an observer, yet one who is *there*. It was very exciting. I saw the big stone longhouse in all its glory, white and new, with posts and doorways and pictures of creatures of all sorts carved in the stone. Birds and snakes and the great spotted jaguars. Men with headdresses of feathers, which looked like that we had seen among the jaguar-men.

The hill itself was new, the stones freshly laid. There was a ceremony in progress, with much chanting and beating of drums and a procession led by ones who seemed to be their holy men. The colors of their robes and headdresses were brilliant. In the procession were those who appeared to be receiving special honor of some sort. They were handsome young men, walking with pride and distinction as they followed the priests up the steps of the man-made hill toward the great white building.

In my dream or vision, I hurried to climb the hill on another side, so that I might see the ceremony more closely and know of its powerful medicine.

The hill was steep, of course, and I struggled to reach the top. It was the helpless feeling of the dream-struggle, where one tries to reach but cannot, or tries to run with feet that will not work. Like that. All around me were the little squirrellike creatures, jumping and chattering as they scampered in the bushes.

Wait . . . the hill had been new and bare and the stones white. But even while I dreamed it, the hill was aging. Trees and vines and bushes had grown up in the cracks between the stones. The dream was becoming mixed, the past and the present, the dreamworld and the real. The chattering that I heard in my dream was really sounding now in my ears.

Day was just dawning. I struggled to open my eyes, not wanting to leave the beauty of the dream and its glorious celebration of the past. I realized, though, that it was time. As I began to recognize my surroundings, I remembered that today I would be permitted to climb the ancient, broken steps. I would see with my own eyes the reality of the big lodge above me. I was now thinking of it as a holy place, a place of worship and powerful spirit-medicine.

I managed to open my eyes fully, now. I was lying on my back and looking straight upward. Not far over my bed was a drooping branch of a large tree. The chattering sound that had been in my dream was now in the real world and seemed to be centered in that one branch. I rubbed my eyes and tried to see, then gasped in astonishment. Peering back at me from the leafy hiding place was a face. I could plainly see the bright little eyes, the nose, lips much like my own. There was a curious expression there, a questioning look that seemed to challenge my presence. It took me only a moment to realize that I was looking into the face of one of the Little People.

I had never before seen one of the Little People. As you know, all tribes and nations tell of their own Little People. For some, they are dangerous, for some, helpful. Maybe both. Sometimes they are tricksters. I have even heard of a tribe in which, if one sees one of their Little People, he must never admit it or he dies!

Now among our Elk-dog People, we have legends of Little People, but they are not a big part of our tradition. Sometimes someone talks of them, but not very seriously. Once I heard a man insist that he had seen one, but he was a little bit crazy anyway. But enough . . .

My friends, this little man was real! I could plainly see his little brown fingers grasping the branch. He was looking directly into my face, and his eye widened when he saw that I was awake.

I gasped and sat up, half afraid. Well, maybe more than half. The little man opened his mouth and screamed at me. I could see his long sharp teeth, and I remembered the stories of dangerous encounters. Then he gave a shout which I took to be a cry of warning, and quickly retreated, swinging with ease from branch to branch. Now came an even more amazing thing. Others of the Little People seemed to appear from nowhere. Several were in the very tree under which I had slept! They all retreated in the same direction, toward the hill with the stone medicine lodge. In the space of a few heartbeats they had disappeared, leaving only the slight swinging movements of the bushes as evidence of their passing.

Now I was taken completely by surprise. I suddenly realized that the creatures we had seen and heard at dusk were not like squirrels at all. *We had seen and heard the Little People!*

I was interested, but afraid, too. Was this hill and its lodge the home of the Little People and their mysteries? There was something puzzling here. They did not appear in my dream until I began to wake. No, I *did* dream of the builders of this hill, and the Little People were not part of it. It must be that after the Old Ones were gone, the Little People came. Were they the reason the Old Ones left? *Aiee,* this might be a dangerous place! Yet White Flower seemed to think of no danger. I rose quickly to seek her and ask of these things.

I was amazed, then, when she laughed at me! I had

rushed over to her as she wakened and signed, rather excitedly.

"I have seen the Little People!"

Flower looked irritated for a moment, as if she resented my rousing her from sleep. Then she looked puzzled, and finally howled with laughter. I did not understand, and asked Caddo Talker, who was sleeping next to her, to interpret.

Then it became really confusing. You would have to be there to understand, and even then you would not. At least, *I* did not. You see, in our tongue, "Little People" means . . . well, the Little People. We understand when someone says that. But after translating through Caddo and Flower's tongue and back again, we find that when Flower says "little people" or "little men" it is not the same as what we call the Little People. These are animals, she told us, and the name they are called is "little men." Her people do not fear them. They even kill and eat them sometimes, she said. (This did not surprise me, knowing the cannibal customs of others in the region.)

Well, I had my doubts. I had seen the face of the little man who looked into mine. He was real, and he did not appear to me to be an animal. The others were impressed, too. Flower suggested, half teasing, that if we had doubts we should kill one and look at it. No one was bold enough to do so.

We watched them most of that day, swinging in the treetops and scolding our presence there. They wore no clothes, even breech-clouts. They appeared to be one big family, several males and females, though not in pairs. Some of the little women had young, which they held in their arms to put to breast. Older children would ride on their mothers' backs sometimes.

They were hairy, except for the face. What? How big? Maybe half as tall as a man, if they stood up. Oh! Did I mention that they had tails? Do not laugh, it is true! A long, hairy tail, as long, maybe longer, than their legs. It is a grasping tail, like that of the possum, but hairy. They can hang by it, from a branch. No, you must believe me. Blue Jay will tell you, too, when he recovers.

Now, if you believe me, my friends, you are wondering: Are these animals, as Flower said? Or is this a strange southern race of the Little People? I do not know. And I do not understand.

But I saw them, watched them. They are much like us. They have a face like ours, ears and eyes and a nose and mouth. I was made to think that they frown and smile, are happy and angry and sad, as we are. Their hands have fingers and a thumb. Their feet are different, it is true. More like another hand. But look how they use them: for swinging in trees. The feet are *used* like a hand.

I could not see their lodges well. They are built of leaves and sticks, high in treetops.

They are full of mischief, and stole some of our supplies. This leads me to think of the trickster Little People in the stories of some tribes that we know.

It is true, they are much like animals. The tail . . . I cannot argue that. And the hairy bodies. But look! Many of the whites that we have seen have hairy bodies, do they not? The first ones were *called* Hairfaces, both Spanish and later, French. Even some of the People have some facial hair, said to be inherited from Heads-Off, who brought the First Horse. Many claim this with pride.

Why do these Little People show themselves so readily? I do not know. They do disappear, or hide very readily. Maybe they can become invisible. Sometimes it seemed so.

Are they a spirit-being, as our Little People are? Or animal? Or is there really any difference?

There are many things, my friends, that I do not understand. There are more now than before I went on this journey to the south. But there are many things that I do not have to understand. I do not understand what makes the grass green, or a flower open its blossom, or the geese migrate in the Moon of Falling Leaves. But I know that it happens. There are many things of the spirit that we are not meant to understand, only to enjoy.

Now, about these Little People. I am made to think that there are many kinds of Little People, as there are of other people. There are Growers and Hunters and Forest People and those who catch fish. These look different and speak different tongues and eat different foods. They have different spirits, different stories. Each tribe tells of its own Little People, who are different for each tribe. Some are seldom, maybe *never* seen. But apparently, those of the far south are easily seen. They speak a strange tongue, but so do the people there. The people think of them as animals, but what is the difference? The people there kill and eat each other, too.

I am prepared to admit that these are far different from the Little People of our legends. At least, I think so. I have never seen one of ours. I would imagine ours to look more like us, but smaller. No tails, probably. I would expect ours to be more of a spirit-being.

But I do not know. The thing that I *do* know is the truth that I say to you now. There *are* Little People. Sometimes I have doubted it, but that is a weakness on my part. Now, I have seen them, the Little People of the southern forests.

21

In the excitement of the Little People, I had almost forgotten my wish to climb to the great white medicine lodge. But, I did wish to do so. I mentioned this the next morning, and the others were curious, too. All of us decided to go, including White Flower. It would be safe, she said, to leave our belongings below at the fire.

"But do not leave any food," she cautioned. "The little men . . ."

I thought this rather odd. Our Little People might do much mischief, play many tricks, but I never heard of their stealing food. This reinforced my idea that there must be many tribes of Little People, with different characteristics. Ours are wise, for instance, wiser than humans. These did not seem very smart. Also, I know of no others with tails . . . but enough.

We climbed the steep side of the man-made hill, with the Little People hooting and scolding in their own strange tongue and scampering among the bushes and vines. They are very agile, using arms and legs as well as their tails to swing from tree to tree. It was apparent that the stone lodge on the hilltop was now their home.

I asked Flower if they were related to the Old Ones, and she laughed, long and hard. Again, she reminded me that they are animals. They are simply living, she said, in the empty structure. I do not know. Her people, I think, may be descended from the Old Ones who built this great medicine lodge, but I do not know that, either. If they are, they have lost much. But I am getting ahead of myself again.

We reached the top, out of breath, and found ourselves walking on a flat stone floor in front of the entrance. The spirit-presence of the Old Ones was very strong here. I was drawn to it, longing to know the things that they had known. How, for instance, had they brought these great blocks of stone up this hill? And why? How had they carved them? I could study the carvings now up close. They were remarkably detailed, rounded as if they had been carved of wood with a metal knife. How were these figures carved in stone? And the even greater mystery, *why?* This must be a place of worship, I thought.

There was a big block of stone, square and straight, and I thought from its position that it was probably aligned to the Real-star. Yes! The Old Ones must have had their eyes turned to the sky, and to the spirit-world above. What deities did they worship?

Somehow I realized that this block in front of the medicine lodge must be a place of sacrifice. Our medicine lodge is in a different place each year, because our Sun Dance is so. We move our dwellings. But suppose we did not? We, too, might build a permanent lodge for the Sun Dance. I am not saying that I wish to do this, my brothers. I am only trying to imagine the customs of these wise people, the Old Ones of White Flower's country. I offered a pinch of tobacco on their altar, in honor of their unknown and perhaps forgotten gods. I thought it good to do so.

I returned to my thoughts and to the idea of these people as sky watchers. Maybe *that* was the purpose of this towering hill. A place from which to watch. I still stood beside the altar stone and turned to look across treetops and hills . . . *aiee*, what a distance I could see! I swept the horizon with my eyes.

Then I gasped in surprise. There, far to the west, I could see a column of smoke ascending into the air. It was big, my friends, broad and tall, rising straight upward from the mountains. More accurately, from *a* mountain.

"The Smoking Mountain!" I heard myself whisper.

"What?" asked Flower. "What did you say?"

"Is that the Smoking Mountain?" I asked in hand-signs.

"Of course," she told me, laughing. "Is it not as I said?"

I was too overwhelmed to deny it, even had it not been true.

"Can we go there?" I asked.

My mind was whirling with new thoughts. Was there a connection of some sort between the medicine lodge where we stood and the Smoking Mountain? Was it possible that this hill had been built for the purpose of watching the mountain? I did not know. I *still* do not.

Flower was laughing.

"You can go, maybe," she signed. "It would take many days."

"How many?"

She shrugged. "Many." She showed fingers quickly that indicated most of a moon.

I was disappointed. I was curious about this smoking mountain, and would have wished to go there. That is, if it could be done in two or three days. I also wished to learn more of these Old Ones and their medicine lodge–observation hill. But I knew that our journey had already gone on far too long. There was no way I could justify another two moons . . . one to Smoking Mountain and another back, before even starting home. Even Blue Jay, with his enthusiasm for exploration, would not understand that.

And even now, the others were restless. They had finished looking at the stone medicine lodge and were ready to leave. I wanted to linger a little while, to try to talk with the spirits of the great holy men whose power had inspired this mighty lodge. Flower seemed to sense my concern. This was a very sensitive woman.

"Walks in the Sun," she said, "my people are less than a day from here. You could stay here, and the others can rejoin you tomorrow as you all start back."

I started to say no, to insist that we stay together, but I was greatly tempted. I wanted to see for myself whether my feeling was right, that this medicine lodge was oriented to the Real-star in the north and faced Sun's rising in the east. Then, too, I longed to see the sky at night from the top of this hill, which might have been made for that purpose. The moon . . . it should be nearly full tonight. What a sight it should be from this vantage point! And the Smoking Mountain . . . what would it look like at night? Would its fire be visible, as well as its smoke? Was that the purpose here?

"Your people are that near?" I signed.

"Yes! I thought we might see some of them by now. But my village is near. We will spend the night with them tonight."

I hesitated.

"Ask Blue Jay," she suggested.

"Ask me what?" said Jay, who happened to look around just then.

"She is suggesting that I stay here and wait for you," I told him. "Her people are less than a day from here."

"*Aiee!* So close?"

"Yes, so she tells us. I was wishing that I had more time to talk to the spirits of this place."

Blue Jay thought a moment.

"Well," he said finally, "why not, if you wish?"

It seemed like the chance of a lifetime, to be alone there, to try to reach out to the ancient holy men who had carried out their rituals and chants and ceremonial dances here.

"It is good," I said finally. "But let me cast the bones to be sure."

For whatever reasons, I cannot tell, but I had brought some of my medicine-things with me to the top of the hill. Maybe I had wanted something like this.

My hands were sweating as I spread the skin on which I would toss the bones. I spread it directly on the ancient place of sacrifice, wondering as I did so whether that might anger the old gods. Then I thought better of it, removed my medicine-skin and spread it on the flat stones *beside* the altar. I wished that the others were not there to watch, but I decided it would not interfere with the ceremony. It would only make *me* uncomfortable.

I shook the box, and tossed the bright-colored stones, bits of bones, and carved fetishes of wood and stone across the painted skin. As always, I was fascinated to watch them skitter and jump. It always seems to me that for a moment they take on a life of their own. No matter . . . They came to rest, and I began to try to read th r meaning. How this is done, I cannot tell you, of course. And this cast was even more difficult to read than most. The heavier stone fetishes, which carry farther . . . no . . . but let me tell you this: In all, the signs were good. There were signs of learning and knowledge. Some warning of sickness, which I took to mean that we should continue to take the tea as Flower had taught us.

I could not interpret one strange dark trend which seemed to be associated with learning or something of the sort. But overall, the signs were good.

"It is good," I announced, "I will stay here."

Blue Jay nodded and turned to the others.

"Let us go," he said. Then he turned back to me. "We will see you tomorrow, Walks in the Sun."

I was soon alone.

I sat that evening, watching the moon rise, leaning my back against one of the massive pillars of the Ancient Ones' medicine lodge. I had thought of making my bed directly against the altar stone, but decided against it. It did not seem right, somehow, and I did not want to take the chance that I might offend the spirits there.

I had brought all my possessions, my pack, robes, food, and extra moccasins. I had a small fire. Flower had advised it. Not so much to ward off any dangerous hunters like the big spotted cats, she said. Mostly, it would keep the Little People from stealing my food. Again, I thought this strange.

"They do not have fire?" I asked.

"Of course not!" She laughed.

Maybe she was right. Maybe they *are* animals, and not really "Little People" like ours, but we took no chances. We tried not to offend them.

The moon was full and blood-red as it rose that night. Beautiful! You know sometimes how it seems you hate to go to sleep? The night is alive with mystery, and we are afraid we might miss something. It was like that.

The moon changed from red to silver as it rose, silvering the stone medicine lodge, nearly as bright as day. I could see the tops of trees below me in the forested areas, and heard the cries of the night creatures. I could not see the Smoking Mountain. Was I afraid? Yes, of course, a little bit. It would be foolish not to be. But I did not know the source of my fear. The real danger, that from the hunters of the night? That was probably slight. Or did I dread, just a little, the spirits of the Old Ones? Both, maybe.

I did not know, of course, when I fell asleep, or when I started to dream. It was somewhat as before, the night-vision. I was still sitting, my back against the stone, still feeling its warmth from the afternoon sun. But it had become day now. I had not wakened, you see, but it was day in my dream.

As before, I saw the splendor of a ceremonial procession, the holy men in their colorful robes and headdresses of feathers and the yellow metal. There was a young man, tall, handsome, and proud, who walked among them, wearing a simple white robe. He was to be honored, I thought.

This procession climbed the steps of the hill. Did I say that in my dream the hill was bright and new, the stones square and true? Yes, the hill and the medicine lodge were new. No trees and bushes grew there . . .

I could not see well what was going on, so I rose. Now, since this was a dream, when I say I rose, I really *rose* . . . into the air like a bird. I found myself hovering over the altar as the priests surrounded it and the young man in white approached. It took me a moment to understand what was happening as he laid aside his robe to lie down on the stone slab. Then I realized: *He* was the sacrifice.

At that point I wished that I could waken. I knew I was dreaming, of course, but I was held fast to the scene. I could not take my eyes away. I tried forcibly to escape from that dreamworld, but was dragged back into it, and lost the sense that it was a dream, even. It was *real*, and I am made to think it really *was*. It *did* happen, though I do not know when.

I watched with horror as four priests held the young man's wrists and ankles to assist him in lying still. The leader of the holy men lifted a stone knife, held it to the sky as the chanting reached a climax, and then plunged it into the bare chest before him. Not the heart, though. That was the strange thing. The knife was swift and sure, and in a few heartbeats, it seemed, he plunged his hands and the stone knife inside the chest cavity. Quickly, his hands emerged, holding the bloody, still-beating heart of the handsome young man. The priest held it high, and the chanting became a roar in my ears. . . .

22

I woke, and it was dawn. My body was covered with sweat, in spite of the chill of the night. The roaring I had heard in my dream continued, and I realized now that it was not the crowd below the altar, but the Little People in the trees below me. *Aiee*, they can be loud.

But I was shivering, not from cold but from the enormity of what I had seen. I wished that I had *not*, really. Now my head was whirling with mixed thoughts, and I felt sad. Betrayed, almost. It had been thrilling to feel the wisdom of the Old Ones of this strange place. Many things I would have wished to ask them. How could they build a *hill*, how did they move the great blocks of stone, how and why was their medicine lodge placed here? Did it have something to do with the Smoking Mountain, or only with their observation of the skies? Or both, maybe.

I still wished to know these things. I still do, but it was not to be. I had seen the other side of that great nation and its ways. The dark side. That part I still do not understand, either. There had been revealed to me some of their mysteries, but not enough to know of their ways.

I thought of the beauty of the night, with the rising moon lighting the treetops below me, before I fell asleep. It had been a glimpse of the beauty that they had seen . . . the Old Ones. The Smoking Mountain, too, though we never saw it up close. That, too, was a thing of powerful spirit, a beautiful sight of its own.

I am made to think that these Ancient Ones were a people who found great beauty in their forests, hills, and mountains. The beauty in their carved stone and in the garments they used in the ceremony that I saw in my dream.

Yes, they probably saw beauty in the sacrificial death of their young men, though it would not be so for us. The young man in my dream seemed glad and proud to approach the stone where he gave up his heart and his life. *Aiee*, it is a strange thing. But let me go on.

As I said, it was morning. The wind was still, and to the distant west I could see the black smoke of the Smoking Mountain. It rose straight up for a little, and then bent to drift away. It was a long way from where I stood, and I still wondered at it. But I was willing to leave it behind. I now knew much more about the Old Ones, more than I really wanted to know.

Suddenly, I wanted to go home. That was more important than anything to me. I was impatient for the others to return so that we could leave. Quickly, I gathered my few things and made my way down the steps of the hill. The Little People chattered and howled at me from the trees, and for a moment I thought that maybe they were giving me a message, taunting me for my failure to relate to all of this. *"It is more than you can understand!"* their cries seemed to shout at me. I tried to console myself with the thought that they had been here in touch with the spirits of the Old Ones for a very long time, and they had done nothing at all. They had let the knowledge rot away and fall to ruin. These were not very smart Little People, I think.

It was midday when the others returned. They were happy and full of joy and they carried provisions for our journey home. Several tall warriors were with them, a sort of honor, to see us on our way.

"How is it with you?" White Flower asked me in hand-signs.

"It is good. I have learned much."

She smiled, and I saw great understanding in her eyes. As I said, this was a very perceptive woman. She knew something of my feelings. There was a sort of sympathy in her eyes.

"There is much that my people do not know of the Old Ones," she now signed. "They must have been very wise."

I only nodded. It was too big, too complicated to start a hand-sign conversation. Still, I knew that there must have been holy men among Flower's people who had experienced dreams like mine. I was made to think that Flower knew, too, but we did not speak further of it. There was no need.

"Let us go on," I said. I was ready to leave this place. *Aiee,* how attractive the Sacred Hills would have looked to me just then!

215

"It is good," said Blue Jay. "Flower's brothers will go with us a little way."

I do not know whether these were really her brothers, or kinsmen, or just men of her people. The old problem of language, you know. But it did not matter.

They traveled with us that day and camped with us that night before turning back. I noticed that Flower stayed close to Caddo Talker and slept next to him that night. They had become very close because of the manner in which we had been forced to communicate. He would miss her, I knew. I would, too, I realized, though in a different way. She had been uncomplaining and even cheerful when times were bad, and had been quite helpful. She had saved our lives more than once. With the medicine-tea, and earlier . . . yes, we would have tried to fight the jaguar-men, and would have been killed and eaten. We would all miss her. I wished the best for her. I wanted to tell her that, so I sought her out as we broke camp.

"To meet you has been good," I signed. "May your path be easy now."

She laughed, the delightful trickling laugh that we had all come to love.

"Thank you, Uncle," she signed, "but my path is yours. I go with you. May it be easy for us all."

I was astonished.

"But why? You wished to come home."

"That is true. But that was before I knew Caddo Talker. I am to be his wife."

I was completely surprised, but pleased. It would be good to have her pleasant and helpful company on the long journey home. I had wondered if we could communicate well enough without her. Besides, I was happy both for her and Caddo Talker.

"It is good. My heart is good for you both," I told her.

"Thank you, Uncle," she signed, just a trifle misty-eyed, maybe. "That is important to me."

I do not know why that should be, except that I think she had come to regard me as a father. No, more like an older brother, maybe. Anyway, our spirits met well, and I was glad for her. For her husband, too. I sought him out.

"Caddo Talker," I said, "my heart is good for you. Flower has told me of your good luck."

He was pleased, and we talked of it a little. I was made to think that this was right for both of them, and I was glad. I could see that this woman would be one who would be respected and prized among the plains people. It was good.

Flower's kinsmen or brothers or whatever they were turned back. We turned again toward the gradually sloping trail that led back toward the sea. I approached this with mixed emotions. Travel would be easier when we reached the open seacoast. When we recovered our horses, even faster. But meanwhile, we must pass through the bad-spirit swamps, and the place where brave men are skinned and eaten. All the dangers we had encountered on the journey south, in fact, must now be faced on the way back. It was not a good thought.

I was mostly worried, though, about the swamp-spirits that had killed our brothers. We could fight snakes and thunder-lizards and big spotted cats. Even men who want to eat us. But it is hard to fight things unseen, things of the spirit, like the hot-cold illness. Maybe I dreaded that because I have no medicine that will help it. We must rely on White Flower's skill with the bark tea. We paused long enough to gather a good supply before moving on into the low country. Flower said we must all drink it every day, and we were glad to do so.

There were five of us now, you remember. Blue Jay, Lean Antelope, Caddo Talker and Flower, and myself. Looking at this group, I felt that we could all travel well together with no disagreements.

In spite of my dread, we passed through the lowlands with no problems. The weather was a little drier, there were not so many mosquitos, and we had few difficulties of any kind. We were all careful not to say anything about it, though. That might destroy what we had.

We reached the coast and it felt like a time for rejoicing. It was hard not to become overconfident. We agreed, however, to move as quickly as we could when the weather permitted. I still hoped to follow the springtime into the plains. It pleased me to think that we might enjoy the time of Awakening for more than one moon.

We settled into the routine of travel very quickly. In many ways it was much easier with only five than it had been with the larger party. We had only one fire at night, instead of the two or three that we had had before. Only one, that is, except in areas where the great spotted cats cried their hunting calls into the jungle. Then we built three fires and slept in the middle. We slept closer together then, too. Except for Caddo Talker and Flower, who *always* slept close together.

When we came to the place where our brother had been killed with the blowgun, we were very cautious. We knew that we were at their mercy if they chose to do us harm, so it was no use to try to hide. We boldly built a big fire on the shore, and showed ourselves plainly during the time we were in the area. I felt that we were being watched all the while, but we did not see any sign of the jaguar-men. I think that they did not want to bother with us. Maybe, though, they felt a little sorry over the three men we had lost when we last met. Whatever the reason, we had no contact with them at all on the return journey.

We moved on, sure that the worst was behind us. Our spirits were high, and our confidence was growing.

Maybe we became too confident.

23

"**B**ut where are they? Is this not where we left them?"

We were standing at the meadow where we had left the horses. It was empty.

"I am sure this is the place," Blue Jay insisted.

Caddo Talker was speaking with Flower and now turned back to us.

"She says yes, this is the right place, where we left them."

"Then where are they? Have they all been stolen or eaten by the spotted cats?" Lean Antelope wondered.

"I think not," said Blue Jay. "Let us consider this a little. Snake-Road would have been able to track them. *Aiee,* we miss his skill! But let us try. Spread out across the meadow, look for droppings, and how old they are. Look for grass or browse that has been grazed. The usual."

That was mostly unneeded detail, but probably a worthwhile reminder. We had relied heavily on our tracker, and now must return to using our own powers of observation. We started slowly across the meadow, moving from the beach inland. I noticed a pile of horse droppings, but they were old, crumbling away to dust. Many moons . . .

There was a cry from Antelope, who was on my left.

"*Aiee!*" he called. "Here are bones!"

We gathered at the spot where Antelope stood, and stared at the scattered bones, whitened by sun and rain. They were, without doubt, the bones of a horse. We could clearly see the skull, and a hoof, separated from the toe-bone and lying near.

"The bones are not chewed," observed Blue Jay.

That was good. At least the death of this animal was not from one of the hunting cats or whatever other large predators might live here. The bones were probably stripped by buzzards after the horse died of other causes.

"Is that not the one that was sick?" signed White Flower.

"How can she tell?" asked Jay in astonishment.

Caddo Talker conferred with her for a moment and then explained.

"She says that the hoof over there is striped. She remembered that one of the sick horses was spotted and had striped hooves. It was of interest to her because she had never seen a horse that color."

"That is true," agreed Antelope. "That was the horse of

Dog's Leg, and only those with spotted skin and white around the eyes had striped hooves!"

Once more, I was impressed with this woman.

We searched further, and found the bones of two more horses. There had been only two sick ones, so this was bad news. Another had sickened and died after we left. At least one more. Maybe others, which we had not yet found in the tall grass. Our hearts were heavy. It might be that we must walk all the way home. And aside from the sore and aching feet that this would produce, it would take much, much longer.

Now, should we search more, losing more travel time, or go on? We decided to spend the rest of the day, camp there, and then move on in the morning, whether or not we found the horses. I was trying to convince myself that it was not a really bad situation either way. We had located the cache where we left our saddles, and found that the damp and mildew had all but ruined them. At best, it would take some hard work and a lot of tallow to salvage them. At worst, we might have to abandon them, even if we found the horses.

I recalled now that this was not far from the area where the Elk-dog medicine-bit had rusted so badly. I examined it and found that it was so again. The shiny surface was dark with the red stain. I resolved to spend the evening polishing it and using some ritual that I reserve for such things. *Aiee*, that is a terrible country, my friends. I longed to put it behind me.

Before evening we had found another scattered set of bones, and yet another. We were sure, now, that all the horses were lost. We were on foot.

Yet there was to be another surprise. As we gathered

dejectedly around our fire just before dark, Antelope suddenly lifted his hand.

"Listen!" he whispered.

For a few moments there were only the night sounds of insects and birds. Then came again the cry that had drawn Antelope's attention. It was some distance away, beyond the fringe of forest that ringed our seaside meadow. It was a sound that we had not heard in a long time. Never was a sound so welcome—the unmistakable whinny of a horse!

It was remarkable how our spirits lifted. We now knew that at least one of our horses had survived. There was little sleep that night, and by dawn's first light we were searching. We pushed through the strip of trees and found that beyond was another meadow. It was slightly larger, had better grass, and the stream that had furnished water curled around it in a very pretty way. It was good. Even better, the sight of a little band of horses, heads up, ears forward, looking at us.

There were six of them, and we recognized them all. Apparently they had removed themselves from their dying brothers. Have you ever noticed, my friends, how most animals avoid their own dead? Why, I do not know, but *they* do.

Now the animals approached us, a bit unsure. They were hard to catch, but that was good. All appeared healthy and spirited, rather than slow and dejected. They were fat and sleek.

It took a little while to catch the first one, but once that was done, the rest were easier. One, a spotted mare, resisted all attempts.

"Let her go!" yelled Blue Jay in disgust. "We do not need her anyway."

So it was done. It took most of that day to salvage

saddles and to clean and grease them with animal fat that we had saved for the purpose. We needed only five, of course. That was a good thing, because the rest were so rotten that they were beyond help.

We spent another night there, and you can be sure that we picketed the horses instead of turning them loose. Very early we were on the move. The spotted mare that we had been unable to catch followed us.

"We should have used her for a pack horse!" chuckled Blue Jay.

But, of course, we could not catch her, and if we had, we would have had no pack saddle. I mention this only because that mare continued to follow us. It was nearly a moon later, much farther north, that we were able to trade her to some Caddoes for supplies. That was useful, since it prevented us from being forced to hunt for food, and saved us many days' travel time. By that time, of course, the mare was much gentler. But I get ahead of my story again.

I do not remember how long we traveled after we recovered the horses, before we met more trouble. And this trouble, my friends, nearly destroyed us. We had nearly forgotten the thing that Flower had told us, that the hot-cold sickness sometimes waits a long time to strike again. What a devious way for an illness to strike!

We were all sick, all but Flower. We had stopped taking the tea after we reached a point where she had thought it safe. I feared that there was no more of the medicine bark, but that was not true. This remarkable woman had actually saved some back for just such an event. Caddo Talker was the first to sicken, and we stopped to make a more permanent camp so that we could care for him. I was next, then Blue Jay and finally, Antelope. White Flower cared for us all, cooking, preparing her tea, wiping fevered brows, and talking softly to us as one would to a child.

Some were much sicker than others, as we had noticed before. I also felt that I was getting to know this spirit and how to treat it. Too much of the tea makes the stomach very sick, too little does not help the chills and fever. Why did Flower not fall ill? I do not know, but I am made to think that it is because she *knows* this spirit, from long contact. They are still enemies, but have agreed on peace. Anyway, she did not sicken the whole time we were in the region of those hot-cold spirits.

My one concern as I began to recover was that we would run out of the medicine bark. What would happen then? Flower assured me not to worry, but I saw a look of concern in her face. I thought that she must be nearing the end of the supply. As it turned out, it was a very close thing. When she stopped giving the tea to Antelope she had barely enough left for a few days.

We moved on when we were able, though we were all very weak. We reached the village where we had bought Flower, and found that the man who had had some claim on her was still not very happy about it. For a little while, I thought that Caddo Talker would try to fight him. That was not a good idea, because he was still very weak. The hot-cold illness takes a long time.

We solved the problem by trading the spotted mare . . . yes, that is where! That food allowed us to move on, and we were able to find the band of Head Splitters to which Caddo Talker belonged. That was many days later, of course.

We were welcomed warmly by these, our allies, who wished to hear of our adventures. We were taken into the lodges of Caddo Talker's family. They called him Bear's Head, of course. His mother welcomed White Flower as a daughter, and they soon began plans for a lodge for the new couple. The rest of us stayed in the lodge of Caddo Talker's sister. She was a beautiful woman. Our hearts were heavy for her, because she was just over her period of mourning for her husband, killed in last year's hunt. She had a small child. She moved into her mother's lodge and we used the empty one, because it would not be good . . . well, you understand.

We recovered very slowly, especially Blue Jay. He was struck down very hard. But he wanted to go home, and as soon as he could ride, he insisted that we move on. We could tell that spring was coming to the plains ahead of us, and we started northward, following the geese.

We hoped to reach the People by the time of the Sun Dance.

24

What? How did Lean Antelope die? *Aiee*, he is not dead! Did I not tell you? I guess no one asked. He has no family? Ah, yes, I remember. He lived in his mother's lodge, but she had died that summer. Of course! That was why he decided to go with us.

Well, he is not dead. But he decided to stay with the Head Splitters, at least for a season. Why? You see, he and the pretty sister of Caddo Talker were becoming very close. He wanted to court her, but there were many young men with the same idea. He decided to stay. We will hear of it, probably at the Sun Dance next year, because I am sure that Caddo Talker and Flower will attend, to see us again. And if he fails in his courtship, he will probably come home sooner.

All of the others . . . gone. The two who left us? Yes, you have told me they did not return. As I look back, this journey was a terrible thing. So many useless deaths. *Aiee*, we have fought battles where we had fewer killed.

And in another way, maybe we have learned much. We saw many strange things. Some were evil, nearly all were frightening. Well, not all. The little armored possum, the no-mouth eater of ants. Those were amusing. I was interested in the tooth-fish, though I hope never to see one alive. Other things . . . the bright parrots, the great lizards of the swamp . . . the spotted hunting cats, and of course, the man-eating men.

Some things I would like to see again. No, I do not want to go back. At least, not now. But there are things that make me want to learn. The Ancient Ones who built the medicine hill and the great lodge on its top. I envy their wisdom and their accomplishments. I have wondered many times: Where did they go, and why? Was there something about their gifts or their use of them that blocked further knowledge? Maybe they misused it. Theirs was certainly a great gift of the spirits. And the greater the gift, the greater the danger to one who misuses it. Did that destroy them? Maybe.

I think also of the Little People. There is something very different about them. I am sure that they are not like our Little People. Not like us, either. Not human. They have tails, but I am made to think that that has little to do with it. I wonder how smart they really are.

These are some of the things of which I wonder. My greatest disappointment, aside from the tragedy of the deaths, is that of the Smoking Mountain. We saw it only at a very great distance. But, judging from Flower's description, and from how long it would have taken to travel there, it must be far away, and *huge*. My curiosity about a mountain that belches fire is maybe the one thing that might make me go back. Ah, I see the look on the face of my wife, Running Deer. No, no, Deer, I did not mean it that way! *Aiee*, I am in trouble! Just now, there is *nothing* that would make me leave our lodge again.

But again, I say, this journey has been useful. We have answered, at least partly, the question of what lies south of us. A salty ocean, damp forests, many dangers. The grass is not reliable, after a certain point.

There are people who live there, but their ways are not ours. We are children of the prairie, the grassland. We are hunters of buffalo. The Sacred Hills, where we have lived for many lifetimes, are nourished with our blood, as we are nourished by their grasses, through the flesh of the buffalo. And it is good.

There may be reason sometimes for us to travel, to move into other areas for special purposes. But even as we do so, I hope that we can remember our heritage. Our place is here. Our world is the sun, the grass, and the buffalo. Now, when the Keeper of the Sacred Bundle announces it, let us enjoy the Sun Dance.

My friends, I will give thanks for my return. I now know much more of who I am, and where I belong.

I am *home*.

Epilogue

▼▼▼

T he account of the journey to the south, as related by Walks in the Sun, was retold many times in later years. It became an epic in the legendry of the People.

Blue Jay was never the same again. Not only was his prestige gone, but so was his will to live. He did attend the Sun Dance ceremonies, but did not participate actively. As one of the older women said, clucking her tongue in sad disapproval, his spirit was dying. His wife remained loyal to him, caring for him as his spirit drained away and his health further declined. He could not take part in the Fall

Hunt, and he died, perhaps appropriately, in the Moon of Madness, just before the Long Nights' Moon. His wife faithfully performed the ceremony of mourning. The following year at the Sun Dance she married a rising young subchief of the Red Rocks band, and the People were happy for them.

Also at that Sun Dance, visitors came from the Head Splitters. Among them were Bear's Head, known to the People as Caddo Talker, and his beautiful wife from a Southern tribe. With them, Lean Antelope, who had married the sister of Caddo Talker. The two couples seemed very close, and after that, often spent a season with Antelope's people. Neither of these men developed any political ambitions, but were regarded as friends by everyone and respected for their bravery.

Walks in the Sun rose in prominence and is still remembered as one of the greatest of holy men.

In later years, no one could recall how certain designs and imagery had become incorporated into the symbolic art of the People. A giant lizard and a great fish, both with many sharp teeth . . . A bird with a hooked beak like an eagle's, but with many bright colors . . . A design like a campfire on the crest of a mountain. Occasionally one of the elders remembered that these things were somehow related to the legend of the exploring party who went too far south.

GENEALOGY

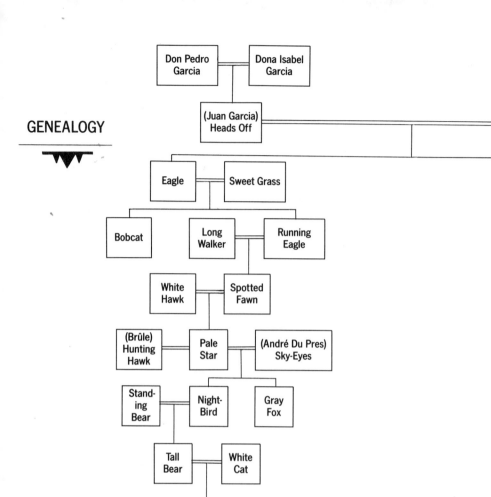

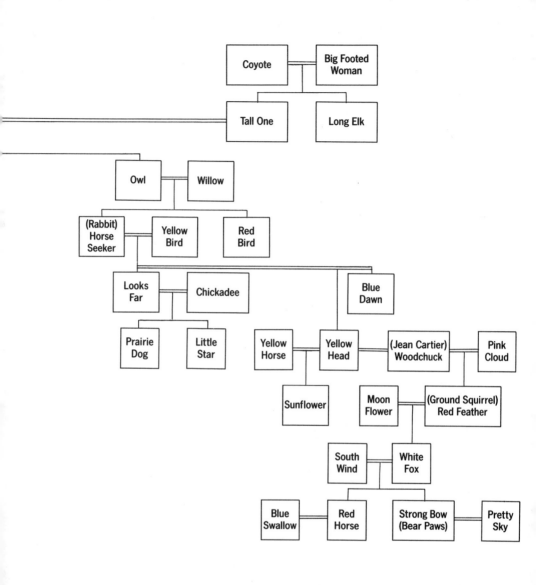